DAWN O'HARA, THE GIRL WHO LAUGHED

AN EDNA FERBER NOVEL

By

EDNA FERBER

WITH AN INTRODUCTION
BY ROGERS DICKINSON

First published in 1911

Read & Co.

Copyright © 2022 Read & Co. Classics

This edition is published by Read & Co. Classics,
an imprint of Read & Co.

This book is copyright and may not be reproduced or copied in any way without the express permission of the publisher in writing.

British Library Cataloguing-in-Publication Data
A catalogue record for this book is available
from the British Library.

Read & Co. is part of Read Books Ltd.
For more information visit
www.readandcobooks.co.uk

TO MY DEAR MOTHER
WHO FREQUENTLY INTERRUPTS
AND TO MY SISTER FANNIE
WHO SAYS "SH-SH-SH!" OUTSIDE MY DOOR

CONTENTS

EDNA FERBER
By Rogers Dickinson..................................7

CHAPTER I
THE SMASH-UP...................................19

CHAPTER II
MOSTLY EGGS....................................27

CHAPTER III
GOOD AS NEW 36

CHAPTER IV
DAWN DEVELOPS A HEIMWEH....................44

CHAPTER V
THE ABSURD BECOMES SERIOUS 54

CHAPTER VI
STEEPED IN GERMAN 65

CHAPTER VII
BLACKIE'S PHILOSOPHY..........................74

CHAPTER VIII
KAFFEE AND KAFFEEKUCHEN 85

CHAPTER IX
THE LADY FROM VIENNA 98

CHAPTER X
A TRAGEDY OF GOWNS..........................106

CHAPTER XI
VON GERHARD SPEAKS 115

CHAPTER XII
BENNIE THE CONSOLER..........................122

CHAPTER XIII
THE TEST...133

CHAPTER XIV
BENNIE AND THE CHARMING OLD MAID 142

CHAPTER XV
FAREWELL TO KNAPFS 153

CHAPTER XVI
JUNE MOONLIGHT, AND A NEW
BOARDINGHOUSE 163

CHAPTER XVII
THE SHADOW OF TERROR 171

CHAPTER XVIII
PETER ORME 181

CHAPTER XIX
A TURN OF THE WHEEL 190

CHAPTER XX
BLACKIE'S VACATION COMES 196

CHAPTER XXI
HAPPINESS 201

EDNA FERBER

By Rogers Dickinson

Edna Ferber is an arresting personality. In speech, in appearance, and in manner she stands out clear against the mass.

Anyone who really knows her realizes why her stories, both long and short, reach the understanding and touch the hearts of the readers. One is very likely to say, "Why, I know somebody like that," or "I knew she would do that."

She knows folks, all sorts of people, but she is interested chiefly in people who do things: not the men who run great corporations and control the destinies of thousands of men and women, but the men and women who have jobs, and under that classification come that vast number who run modest households, who struggle to bring up children, who, in fact, form the permanent solid stratum on which our society is built.

She has the large-minded sympathy that makes for understanding of the under dog. She will take French lessons, not only because she wants to study the language, but because a cultivated Frenchman needs money and will not accept charity.

Edna Ferber enjoys a talk with a washwoman and the woman enjoys the talk too...

... She hates pretension and is very likely to speak her mind not only to her intimates but straight to the face of the objectionable person. Sometimes she speaks more strongly than she should, for she is impulsive and quick-tempered, but no one is more generous than she in the acknowledgment of mistakes.

Her letters are characteristic. They just begin. No salutation, no sparring for an opening—they begin at the beginning and when she is through she stops. She just adds her initials.

She stands on her own small feet. If you say to her, "The mantle of O. Henry has fallen on your shoulders" (it has been said with complimentary intent), you will get a flash from her black eyes that will scorch you and a rush of words that will make you wish you were elsewhere. She does not want anyone's else mantle or footgear for that matter—she is herself, Edna Ferber.

Her earlier picturesque, sometimes flippant style, the surprise climaxes, and the short pithy sentences, come from her newspaper experience and not from any influence of O. Henry. The newspaper editor's command is to "tell the story and make it snappy," and it has affected Edna Ferber's style, as it has affected the work of many other writers who grew out of newspaper offices.

Her style has changed as all thoughtful readers must have noticed. The literary form of the Emma McChesney stories is quite different from that of the stories in "Cheerful by Request" and "Gigolo." Read a story in "Roast Beef Medium" and then read "Old Man Minick."

There is a depth and richness, a dignity and soundness, that the earlier works lacked. Yet there is no loss of strength and vital freshness in her later books.

There is a vitality about Edna Ferber that is recognizable the moment she comes into a room. She enters almost with a rush, with a quick, firm step; though she is short, scarcely more than five feet three, I should think, she dominates most groups. Her rather large head with its thick black hair, cropped so one may see the admirable shape of the skull, is held erect. She greets one with a cordiality that is sometimes disarming and she speaks with a curious drawl that seems quite out of character with her forthright nature. What she says is worth listening to, for even the most commonplace occasions bring forth unbromidic speech from Edna Ferber.

As she talks in private conversation so she talks in public. She is a good speech-maker, a good lecturer. Her spoken words have the pungent vitality of her writing and the reading of her own stories makes the characters come alive startlingly.

It may seem strange to those of us who do not make our own living by creative writing that a woman who has made her mark as a reporter and who still occasionally reports a national convention, finds it so hard to write fiction. Edna Ferber has written for newspapers about all sorts of things under every sort of difficult handicap of time and place, and has produced good "copy." Yet her short stories, novels and plays, are slowly and laboriously produced. And when the job is done, so closely has she held her nose to the grindstone, that she is unable to perceive the work as a whole, and realize how good it is.

She once rented an apartment on the lake front in Chicago, her desk facing the blue waters. She was in the midst of her novel, "The Girls." She complained that she could not get on with it, it was hard labor, so hard that in spite of her best efforts she would look at the lake and the trees and the children playing in the street below. Her anxious publisher besought her to turn her typewriter table so she faced the blank wall. She did; and the book was speedily born.

In an article in *The American Magazine*, under the characteristic title of "The Joy of the Job," she tells of her methods of work.

"At the risk of being hated I wanted to state that I've always felt sorry for any woman who could play whenever she wanted to. She never will know how sweet play can be. Chocolate is no treat for a girl in a candy factory. Play is no treat for an idler. My work is such that morning engagements and festive luncheoning are forbidden. On those rare occasions, two or three times a year, perhaps, when I deliberately, and for the good of my soul, break the rule and sneak off down-town for luncheon, the affair takes on the proportions of an orgy. No college girls' midnight fudge spree could be more thrilling. To my unaccustomed eyes the girls in their new hats all look pretty. The matrons appear amazingly well dressed. The men, chatting over their after-luncheon cigarettes, are captains of finance, discussing problems of national import. I refuse to believe what my *vis-à-vis* says about their being cloak-and-suit salesmen whose conversation probably runs thus:

" 'I come into his place at ten this morning and he wouldn't look at my stuff till twelve, and finally I goes up to him, and I says to him, I says, "Looka here, Marx." '

"The very waiters interest me. The 'bus boys are deft, and I refuse to be bothered by their finger nails. The chicken salad is a poem, the coffee a dream, the French pastry a divine concoction.

"When you work three hundred and fifty mornings in the year, a game of golf on the three hundred and fifty-first is a lark. That's one reason why I play so atrociously, I suppose. They who say that work hardens one, or wearies, or dulls, have chosen the wrong occupation, or have never really tasted the delights of it. It's the finest freshener in the world. It's an appetizer. It's a combination cocktail and *hors d'œuvre*, to be taken before playing. It gives color to the most commonplace of holidays. It makes a run through the park a treat. There's very little thrill in a brisk walk if you can brisk-walk from morning until night. But after having sat before a typewriter, or desk, or table, for hours together, to be able to stretch one's legs for a swing of two or three miles—that's living.

"The entire output of my particular job depends upon me. By that I mean that when I put the cover on my typewriter the works are closed. The office equipment consists of one flat table, rather messy; one typewriter, much abused, and one typewriter table; a chunk of yellow copy paper, and one of white. All the wheels, belts, wires, bolts, files, tools—the whole manufacturing scheme of things—has got to be contained in the space between my chin and my topmost hairpin. And my one horror, my nightmare of nightmares, is that some morning I'll wake up and find that space vacant, and the works closed down, with a mental sign over the front door reading:

" 'For Rent. Fine, large empty head. Inquire within.'

"There was one year when there was a sign reading, 'Closed for repairs.' The horror of it is still with me."

In another place she says: "No autobiographical sketch is complete without a statement of ambitions. I have two. I want to be allowed to sit in a rocking chair on the curb at the corner of State and Madison streets and watch the folks go by. And I would fain live on a houseboat in the Vale of Cashmere. I don't know where the Vale of Cashmere is, nor whether it boasts a water course or not."

What a lot she would get out of her view of life from a rocking chair at State and Madison streets!

She complained bitterly once that a certain writer, now opulent and lazy, who knew Chicago from the stockyards to the North Shore, did not use the stuff he had in his head. She felt not so much that he was missing an opportunity, but that he had buried the talent of experience that should have been passed on to others after he had gone.

Though Edna Ferber lives in New York—her apartment faces Central Park—she is not of New York. She knows Chicago, she thinks Chicago, just as Booth Tarkington thinks and knows Indianapolis and would not live wholly away from it. The author of "The Girls," that masterpiece of Chicago, frequently visits the Windy City and sits, metaphorically, at the corner of State and Madison and soaks in the spirit of the city, that city so recently a pioneer town, so lately an effete city. No wonder she finds it fascinating and inexhaustible.

Edna Ferber's apartment is the place where she meets her friends, breakfasts, lunches, dines, and sleeps. It is her rest house, her relaxation. The furnishing of it was an adventure. The choosing of draperies for the windows (there are many facing east), the tints for the walls, and the fabrics for the upholstery, she found an exhilarating venture into the unknown. She has been a hotel dweller, a renter of the homes of other people. But here she is rioting in her own home with her own furniture and hers is the sole responsibility for the color scheme, the style, and the composition. And it is good. Her taste in furnishing as in writing is to be relied upon. It is also most comfortable, too comfortable. It would be hard enough to break away from this interesting woman if one were standing talking in a windy street, but when surrounded by all the comforts it is almost impossible not to overstay one's welcome.

But she works in a bare studio, close by, away from the telephone and too friendly visitors. Every morning she sits down at the typewriter and works—and most afternoons. No writer produces good work without wearying effort, long hours of concentration, and at times great discouragement.

What Miss Ferber wears while she works, whether dress, sweater, or smock, I do not know, for she does not do her writing in public as a prize fighter trains for a battle. Her battles are fought out alone.

One of her old and understanding friends, William Allen White, has written a most illuminating account of her life, her struggles, and her achievement. Mr. White being a Middle Westerner himself, quite understands Edna Ferber's point of view. The following extract is taken from an introduction by the famous editor of the *Emporia Gazette* for an edition of "Cheerful by Request":

"Edna Ferber's pasture is long and narrow geographically; ranging from a thin pennant running westward to the mountains, to a slim tatter as far east as Vienna. But it is close clipped around Chicago, in Illinois, Minnesota, and Wisconsin; and well cropped in and about New York. In its social boundaries her field is more compact; chiefly lying in the middle class, sometimes taking in those who are just climbing out of poverty, and often considering those who are happily wiggling into our plutocracy. But one thread will string every character she ever conceived; all her people do something for a living. She is the goddess of the worker. And from her typewriter keys spring hard-working bankers, merchants, burglars, garage-helpers, stenographers, actors, traveling salesmen, hotel clerks, porters and reporters, wholesalers, pushcart men, wine touts, welfare workers, farmers, writers—always doers of things: money makers, men and women who pull their weight in the boat. And her stories chiefly tell what a fine time these hardworking Americans have with their day's work.

"In the Great American Short Story, which must tell of American life rather than our Great American Novel, Edna Ferber's section will be among the workers. Mrs. Wharton and Henry Fuller and Sherwood Anderson can have the loafers, in high life and low life. But Miss Ferber's people will come from the stores and offices and workshops. They will, as the Gospel Hymn has it, come rejoicing, bringing home the bacon. Their dramatic moments are oftenest in aprons, shirt-sleeves, overalls, at desks, behind counters, in kitchens, behind stage curtains, in the midst of the business of earning a living. Precious little is done in the Ferber stories 'in God's great out of doors—in the wide open spaces.' When anything has to be open in Miss Ferber's work it is a lively and festive wide-open town.

"So let us consider who she is and how she happened to be a writing woman. In the middle or late 'eighties of the nineteenth century she was born in Kalamazoo, Michigan, of Jewish parents. Her father was a Hungarian. Her mother an American, born in Milwaukee, Wisconsin. Her father was the owner of a general merchandise store, first in Iowa, then in Appleton, Wisconsin. Miss Ferber at seventeen was graduated from the Ryan High School in Appleton. For her graduating essay she wrote an account of the life of the women workers in a local mill. The local editor saw it: recognized that it was good reporting and gave her a job as local reporter at $3.00 a week—a rather princely salary twenty years ago for a new girl reporter in a country town. She wrote local items, from the court house, the city hall, the fire department, the home of the village Crœsus, and the police court. Then she was graduated from the Appleton paper to Milwaukee. In Milwaukee also she was a reporter. And while she was earning a living as a reporter she wrote 'Dawn O'Hara,' her first novel. It sold well. While it was in the press and selling during 1911 and '12, the magazines began telling the story of 'Emma McChesney.' Here was something new; the traveling saleswoman—who was rather more woman than merchant, but who was altogether human. The character appealed to the public, and Edna Ferber had her knee in the door of success. In 1913 the stories were collected under the title 'Roast Beef Medium,' and that book sold well. Two years later appeared more McChesney stories under the title 'Emma McChesney & Co.' Then came the play 'Emma McChesney,' and Edna Ferber was well in the ante-room of the hall of fame, with her card going to posterity. In the meantime, a book of short stories, 'Buttered Side Down,' had been written and sold to the magazines and successfully published. In 1917 Miss Ferber's second novel appeared, 'Fanny, Herself,' and in 1918 came 'Cheerful by Request.'

"In 1922 all the promise of ten years of conscientious work was fulfilled, when Miss Ferber wrote 'The Girls,' a novel of Chicago. The humor of it, the strength of it, the art of it, must make posterity give more than a glance at Edna Ferber's card. She has something to tell posterity about America.

"And so we must tell posterity something about her—about Edna Ferber, herself. The best description of her family life ever written, she wrote in the dedication of 'Dawn O'Hara,' to Julia Ferber, her 'dear mother who frequently interrupts, and to Sister Fannie who says Sh-Sh-Sh- outside my door.' Some shadowy hint of the life of the Ferbers after the husband and father died, and before the family moved to Chicago, may be found in the earlier chapters of 'Fanny, Herself'—at least it is a good picture of Julia Ferber, the mother, a strong, devoted, capable woman who is a credit to her country.

"All around Edna Ferber is an atmosphere of work. She works hard and all the time. Her friends work hard, and all the time. So when she takes her typewriter in hand to tell of the world she knows, she describes a working world. It is a world deeply American. For whatever else we Americans are, we are workers.

Here and there a man lives without work, a white rich man's son or a black washerwoman's son. We have no leisure classes. But the world of Edna Ferber's people in its economic status is the real world of America. And she, a working woman, is typical of the modern American woman. If for any reason posterity is interested in this American world of the first three decades of the twentieth century, posterity will do well—indeed posterity probably can do no better than to tell the butler to bring Edna Ferber for a few moments and let her read 'The Gay Old Dog,' and 'The Eldest.' "

Since Mr. White wrote the foregoing, Edna Ferber has made two big steps forward. In the volume, "Gigolo," is to be found that masterpiece, "Old Man Minick," to mention but one of a group of eight. The play from this story, written by her in collaboration with George S. Kaufman, has become an artistic and a financial success. The story, "Old Man Minick," together with the play, "Minick," have been published in a separate volume, so one can see how a short story can be turned into a successful play. It is interesting to compare the fictional use of an idea with the dramatic, especially when the work is done by the same hand.

Edna Ferber has always been interested in plays and playwriting. She has written three that I know of, and two have been highly successful. "$1,200 a Year," written with Newman Levy, deserved a greater success than it won. As a piece of literature it deserves more than one rereading.

Of course "So Big" has done more to interest people in Edna Ferber than anything else, yet the quality that has made such a success of that book lies also in most of her earlier work. That she herself was not too sure about it is made clear in an interview, titled "How it Feels to be a Best Seller":

"There are people who write Best Sellers as a matter of business. That is, they are in the Best Seller business. They write them, I am told, deliberately and mathematically, using a formula as a cook uses a recipe. You hear a name and you say, in your ignorance, 'Who? . . . Who's he?' And the answer is, 'He's Whosis. You don't mean to say you've never read him! He writes Best Sellers.'

"I don't know how they do it. I don't want to know. I suppose they have some peculiar thermometer or mechanism by which they gauge that fickle phenomenon known as the public pulse. But occasionally some one comes along who commits a Best Seller in all innocence, and with no such intent. Of such am I.

"Not only did I not plan to write a Best Seller when I wrote 'So Big' but I thought, when I had finished it, that I had written the world's worst seller. Not that alone, I thought I had written a complete Non-Seller. I didn't think anyone would ever read it. And that's the literal truth.

"It was this way. I had worked on it, day after day, day after day, for many months, starting at nine each morning and working until four in the afternoon. I knew where I was going and why I wanted to get there, but after a time I became like a patient plodder who must travel weary miles along a lonely road before he arrives at the city of his destination. Mile after mile I covered the distance, sometimes traveling fairly swiftly, sometimes scarcely able to lift one tired foot after the other. When it was finished I was so dulled by contact with it that I scarcely could see it. The last stretch of the work, during June and July, had been written in Chicago. That June and July in Chicago I recall as a period during which the thermometer hovered gracefully between 90 and 96 in the shade.

"As the work of final correction began and progressed I began to dole out sheaves of copy to the typist. She used to call for a chunk of the story every day or two. She would appear at about four in the afternoon when I had finished work for the day, and when I was at my limpest, dampest and lowest. I remember her as a nice fresh-looking red-haired girl in crisp cool orchid organdie. She would make four copies of each fresh sheaf as she received it, return these, and call for more. No other soul except myself had seen a line of that story.

"Each time she called I waited eagerly, hopefully, for her to make some comment. I wanted her to say she liked Selina. I wanted her to say she didn't care for Dirk. I wanted her to say she thought the story should have ended this way, or that. I wanted her to evince some interest in the novel; to show some liking for it, or even to show dislike. She never did.

" 'Well,' said I to Miss E. Ferber, 'that settles it. There you are, Edna! I told you so! Who would be interested in a novel about a middle-aged woman in a calico dress and with wispy hair and bad teeth, grubbing on a little truck farm south of Chicago! Nobody. Who cares about cabbages! Nobody. Who would read the thing if it came out as a novel! A dull plodding book, written because I was interested; because I wanted intensely to write it; because I had carried the thought of it around in my head for five years or more.'

"The story was to be serialized in the *Woman's Home Companion* before being published in novel form. Well, that was all right. It might go well enough as a serial. But as a novel! Never.

"I wrote Mr. Russell Doubleday, of Doubleday, Page & Company, telling him that I had finished the book but that it was not, in my opinion, a book that would sell. No one, I wrote him, would read it. I thought it would be better for his firm, as publishers, and for me, as author, if we gave up the idea of publishing this story as a novel. It would be a flat failure, receiving bad reviews, having no sale.

"Mr. Doubleday replied that I might be right, but that perhaps I should let some one besides myself have a chance to judge its merits and faults. Perhaps, he said, I had been too close to it. Would I let him read it before deciding against it?

"He read it. He wrote me a letter. I keep that letter to read on rainy days when I'm not feeling well.

" 'So Big' has, for some reason I can't explain, been a best seller since it was published in February, selling on an average of a thousand a day. I know how the ugly duckling felt who turned into a swan."

And so, unlike Dirk de Jong, who thought he was so big and wasn't, the novel is so very big, when the author thought it of much less importance.

It is safe to say that at least seven million people read "So Big" in its serial and book form. All these people will be looking forward hopefully to her next book. That there will be no disappointment can be confidently predicted because Edna Ferber has built upon so sure a foundation.

I believe that big work cannot come of small people. Edna Ferber is a big person (not in stature nor avoirdupois) in mind, in heart, in soul, and in vision. A study of her work shows her growth and she is still growing, and will keep on growing as long as she lives. She will keep on growing because she sees so much farther than she has been able to reach. Her vision is so big.

DAWN O'HARA

CHAPTER I

THE SMASH-UP

There are a number of things that are pleasanter than being sick in a New York boarding-house when one's nearest dearest is a married sister up in far-away Michigan.

Some one must have been very kind, for there were doctors, and a blue-and-white striped nurse, and bottles and things. There was even a vase of perky carnations—scarlet ones. I discovered that they had a trick of nodding their heads, saucily. The discovery did not appear to surprise me.

"Howdy-do!" said I aloud to the fattest and reddest carnation that overtopped all the rest. "How in the world did you get in here?"

The striped nurse (I hadn't noticed her before) rose from some corner and came swiftly over to my bedside, taking my wrist between her fingers.

"I'm very well, thank you," she said, smiling, "and I came in at the door, of course."

"I wasn't talking to you," I snapped, crossly, "I was speaking to the carnations; particularly to that elderly one at the top—the fat one who keeps bowing and wagging his head at me."

"Oh, yes," answered the striped nurse, politely, "of course.

That one is very lively, isn't he? But suppose we take them out for a little while now."

She picked up the vase and carried it into the corridor, and the carnations nodded their heads more vigorously than ever over her shoulder.

I heard her call softly to some one. The some one answered with a sharp little cry that sounded like, "Conscious!"

The next moment my own sister Norah came quietly into the room, and knelt at the side of my bed and took me in her arms. It did not seem at all surprising that she should be there, patting me with reassuring little love pats, murmuring over me with her lips against my check, calling me a hundred half-forgotten pet names that I had not heard for years.

But then, nothing seemed to surprise me that surprising day. Not even the sight of a great, red-haired, red-faced, scrubbed looking man who strolled into the room just as Norah was in the midst of denouncing newspapers in general, and my newspaper in particular, and calling the city editor a slave-driver and a beast. The big, red-haired man stood regarding us tolerantly.

"Better, eh?" said he, not as one who asks a question, but as though in confirmation of a thought. Then he too took my wrist between his fingers. His touch was very firm and cool. After that he pulled down my eyelids and said, "H'm." Then he patted my cheek smartly once or twice. "You'll do," he pronounced. He picked up a sheet of paper from the table and looked it over, keen-eyed. There followed a clinking of bottles and glasses, a few low-spoken words to the nurse, and then, as she left the room the big red-haired man seated himself heavily in the chair near the bedside and rested his great hands on his fat knees. He stared down at me in much the same way that a huge mastiff looks at a terrier. Finally his glance rested on my limp left hand.

"Married, h'm?"

For a moment the word would not come. I could hear Norah catch her breath quickly. Then—"Yes," answered I.

"Husband living?" I could see suspicion dawning in his cold gray eye.

Again the catch in Norah's throat and a little half warning, half supplicating gesture. And again, "Yes," said I.

The dawn of suspicion burst into full glow.

"Where is he?" growled the red-haired doctor. "At a time like this?"

I shut my eyes for a moment, too sick at heart to resent his manner. I could feel, more than see, that Sis was signaling him frantically. I moistened my lips and answered him, bitterly.

"He is in the Starkweather Hospital for the insane."

When the red-haired man spoke again the growl was quite gone from his voice.

"And your home is—where?"

"Nowhere," I replied meekly, from my pillow. But at that Sis put her hand out quickly, as though she had been struck, and said:

"My home is her home."

"Well then, take her there," he ordered, frowning, "and keep her there as long as you can. Newspaper reporting, h'm? In New York? That's a devil of a job for a woman. And a husband who... Well, you'll have to take a six months' course in loafing, young woman. And at the end of that time, if you are still determined to work, can't you pick out something easier—like taking in scrubbing, for instance?"

I managed a feeble smile, wishing that he would go away quickly, so that I might sleep. He seemed to divine my thoughts, for he disappeared into the corridor, taking Norah with him. Their voices, low-pitched and carefully guarded, could be heard as they conversed outside my door.

Norah was telling him the whole miserable business. I wished, savagely, that she would let me tell it, if it must be told. How could she paint the fascination of the man who was my husband? She had never known the charm of him as I had known it in those few brief months before our marriage. She had never felt the caress of his voice, or the magnetism of his strange, smoldering eyes glowing across the smoke-dimmed city room as I had felt them fixed on me. No one had ever known what he had meant to the girl of twenty, with her brain full of unspoken dreams—dreams which were all to become glorious realities in that wonder-place, New York.

How he had fired my country-girl imagination! He had been the most brilliant writer on the big, brilliant sheet—and the most dissolute. How my heart had pounded on that first lonely day when this Wonder-Being looked up from his desk, saw me, and strolled over to where I sat before my typewriter! He smiled down at me, companionably. I'm quite sure that my mouth must have been wide open with surprise. He had been smoking a cigarette an expensive-looking, gold-tipped one. Now he removed it from between his lips with that hand that always shook a little, and dropped it to the floor, crushing it lightly with the toe of his boot. He threw back his handsome head and sent out the last mouthful of smoke in a thin, lazy spiral. I remember thinking what a pity it was that he should have crushed that costly-looking cigarette, just for me.

"My name's Orme," he said, gravely. "Peter Orme. And if yours isn't Shaughnessy or Burke at least, then I'm no judge of what black hair and gray eyes stand for."

"Then you're not," retorted I, laughing up at him, "for it happens to be O'Hara—Dawn O'Hara, if ye plaze."

He picked up a trifle that lay on my desk—a pencil, perhaps, or a bit of paper—and toyed with it, absently, as though I had not spoken. I thought he had not heard, and I was conscious of feeling a bit embarrassed, and very young. Suddenly he raised his smoldering eyes to mine, and I saw that they had taken on a deeper glow. His white, even teeth showed in a half smile.

"Dawn O'Hara," said he, slowly, and the name had never sounded in the least like music before, "Dawn O'Hara. It sounds like a rose—a pink blush rose that is deeper pink at its heart, and very sweet."

He picked up the trifle with which he had been toying and eyed it intently for a moment, as though his whole mind were absorbed in it. Then he put it down, turned, and walked slowly away. I sat staring after him like a little simpleton, puzzled, bewildered, stunned. That had been the beginning of it all.

He had what we Irish call "a way wid him." I wonder now why I did not go mad with the joy, and the pain, and the uncertainty of it all. Never was a girl so dazzled, so humbled, so worshiped, so neglected, so courted. He was a creature of a thousand moods to torture one. What guise would he wear to-day? Would he be gay, or dour, or sullen, or teasing or passionate, or cold, or tender or scintillating? I know that my hands were always cold, and my cheeks were always hot, those days.

He wrote like a modern Demosthenes, with all political New York to quiver under his philippics. The managing editor used to send him out on wonderful assignments, and they used to hold the paper for his stuff when it was late. Sometimes he would be gone for days at a time, and when he returned the men would look at him with a sort of admiring awe. And the city editor would glance up from beneath his green eye-shade and call out:

"Say, Orme, for a man who has just wired in about a million dollars' worth of stuff seems to me you don't look very crisp and jaunty."

"Haven't slept for a week," Peter Orme would growl, and then he would brush past the men who were crowded around him, and turn in my direction. And the old hot-and-cold, happy, frightened, laughing, sobbing sensation would have me by the throat again.

Well, we were married. Love cast a glamour over his very vices. His love of drink? A weakness which I would transform into strength. His white hot flashes of uncontrollable temper? Surely they would die down at my cool, tender touch. His fits of abstraction and irritability? Mere evidences of the genius within. Oh, my worshiping soul was always alert with an excuse.

And so we were married. He had quite tired of me in less

than a year, and the hand that had always shaken a little shook a great deal now, and the fits of abstraction and temper could be counted upon to appear oftener than any other moods. I used to laugh, sometimes, when I was alone, at the bitter humor of it all. It was like a Duchess novel come to life.

His work began to show slipshod in spots. They talked to him about it and he laughed at them. Then, one day, he left them in the ditch on the big story of the McManus indictment, and the whole town scooped him, and the managing editor told him that he must go. His lapses had become too frequent. They would have to replace him with a man not so brilliant, perhaps, but more reliable.

I daren't think of his face as it looked when he came home to the little apartment and told me. The smoldering eyes were flaming now. His lips were flecked with a sort of foam. I stared at him in horror. He strode over to me, clasped his fingers about my throat and shook me as a dog shakes a mouse.

"Why don't you cry, eh?" he snarled. "Why don't you cry!"

And then I did cry out at what I saw in his eyes. I wrenched myself free, fled to my room, and locked the door and stood against it with my hand pressed over my heart until I heard the outer door slam and the echo of his footsteps die away.

Divorce! That was my only salvation. No, that would be cowardly now. I would wait until he was on his feet again, and then I would demand my old free life back once more. This existence that was dragging me into the gutter—this was not life! Life was a glorious, beautiful thing, and I would have it yet. I laid my plans, feverishly, and waited. He did not come back that night, or the next, or the next, or the next. In desperation I went to see the men at the office. No, they had not seen him. Was there anything that they could do? they asked. I smiled, and thanked them, and said, oh, Peter was so absent-minded! No doubt he had misdirected his letters, or something of the sort. And then I went back to the flat to resume the horrible waiting.

One week later he turned up at the old office which had cast him off. He sat down at his former desk and began to write, breathlessly, as he used to in the days when all the big stories fell to him. One of the men reporters strolled up to him and touched him on the shoulder, man-fashion. Peter Orme raised his head and stared at him, and the man sprang back in terror. The smoldering eyes had burned down to an ash. Peter Orme was quite bereft of all reason. They took him away that night, and I kept telling myself that it wasn't true; that it was all a nasty dream, and I would wake up pretty soon, and laugh about it, and tell it at the breakfast table.

Well, one does not seek a divorce from a husband who is insane. The busy men on the great paper were very kind. They would take me back on the staff. Did I think that I still could write those amusing little human interest stories? Funny ones, you know, with a punch in 'em.

Oh, plenty of good stories left in me yet, I assured them. They must remember that I was only twenty-one, after all, and at twenty-one one does not lose the sense of humor.

And so I went back to my old desk, and wrote bright, chatty letters home to Norah, and ground out very funny stories with a punch in 'em, that the husband in the insane asylum might be kept in comforts. With both hands I hung on like grim death to that saving sense of humor, resolved to make something of that miserable mess which was my life—to make something of it yet. And now—

At this point in my musings there was an end of the low-voiced conversation in the hall. Sis tiptoed in and looked her disapproval at finding me sleepless.

"Dawn, old girlie, this will never do. Shut your eyes now, like a good child, and go to sleep. Guess what that great brute of a doctor said! I may take you home with me next week! Dawn dear, you will come, won't you? You must! This is killing you. Don't make me go away leaving you here. I couldn't stand it."

She leaned over my pillow and closed my eyelids gently with her sweet, cool fingers. "You are coming home with me, and you shall sleep and eat, and sleep and eat, until you are as lively as the Widow Malone, ohone, and twice as fat. Home, Dawnie dear, where we'll forget all about New York. Home, with me."

I reached up uncertainly, and brought her hand down to my lips and a great peace descended upon my sick soul. "Home— with you," I said, like a child, and fell asleep.

CHAPTER II

MOSTLY EGGS

Oh, but it was clean, and sweet, and wonderfully still, that rose-and-white room at Norah's! No street cars to tear at one's nerves with grinding brakes and clanging bells; no tramping of restless feet on the concrete all through the long, noisy hours; no shrieking midnight joy-riders; not one of the hundred sounds which make night hideous in the city. What bliss to lie there, hour after hour, in a delicious half-waking, half-sleeping, wholly exquisite stupor, only rousing myself to swallow egg-nogg No. 426, and then to flop back again on the big, cool pillow!

New York, with its lights, its clangor, its millions, was only a far-away, jumbled nightmare. The office, with its clacking typewriters, its insistent, nerve-racking telephone bells, its systematic rush, its smoke-dimmed city room, was but an ugly part of the dream.

Back to that inferno of haste and scramble and clatter? Never! Never! I resolved, drowsily. And dropped off to sleep again.

And the sheets. Oh, those sheets of Norah's! Why, they were white, instead of gray! And they actually smelled of flowers. For that matter, there were rosebuds on the silken coverlet. It took me a week to get chummy with that rosebud-and-down quilt. I had to explain carefully to Norah that after a half-dozen years of sleeping under doubtful boarding-house blankets one does not so soon get rid of a shuddering disgust for coverings which are haunted by the ghosts of a hundred unknown sleepers. Those years had taught me to draw up the sheet with scrupulous care, to turn it down, and smooth it over, so that no contaminating and woolly blanket should touch my skin. The habit stuck even after Norah had tucked me in between her fragrant sheets. Automatically my hands groped about, arranging the old protecting barrier.

"What's the matter, Fuss-fuss?" inquired Norah, looking on. "That down quilt won't bite you; what an old maid you are!"

"Don't like blankets next to my face," I elucidated, sleepily, "never can tell who slept under 'em last—"

"You cat!" exclaimed Norah, making a little rush at me. "If you weren't supposed to be ill I'd shake you! Comparing my darling rosebud quilt to your miserable gray blankets! Just for that I'll make you eat an extra pair of eggs."

There never was a sister like Norah. But then, who ever heard of a brother-in-law like Max? No woman—not even a frazzled-out newspaper woman—could receive the love and care that they gave me, and fail to flourish under it. They had been Dad and Mother to me since the day when Norah had tucked me under her arm and carried me away from New York. Sis was an angel; a comforting, twentieth-century angel, with white apron strings for wings, and a tempting tray in her hands in place of the hymn books and palm leaves that the picture-book angels carry. She coaxed the inevitable eggs and beef into more tempting forms than Mrs. Rorer ever guessed at. She could disguise those two plain, nourishing articles of diet so effectually that neither hen nor cow would have suspected either of having once been part of her anatomy. Once I ate halfway through a melting, fluffy, peach-bedecked plate of something before I discovered that it was only another egg in disguise.

"Feel like eating a great big dinner to-day, Kidlet?" Norah would ask in the morning as she stood at my bedside (with a glass of egg-something in her hand, of course).

"Eat!"—horror and disgust shuddering through my voice—"Eat! Ugh! Don't s-s-speak of it to me. And for pity's sake tell Frieda to shut the kitchen door when you go down, will you? I can smell something like ugh!—like pot roast, with gravy!" And

I would turn my face to the wall.

Three hours later I would hear Sis coming softly up the stairs, accompanied by a tinkling of china and glass. I would face her, all protest.

"Didn't I tell you, Sis, that I couldn't eat a mouthful? Not a mouthf—um-m-m-m! How perfectly scrumptious that looks! What's that affair in the lettuce leaf? Oh, can't I begin on that divine-looking pinky stuff in the tall glass? H'm? Oh, please!"

"I thought—" Norah would begin; and then she would snigger softly.

"Oh, well, that was hours ago," I would explain, loftily. "Perhaps I could manage a bite or two now."

Whereupon I would demolish everything except the china and doilies.

It was at this point on the road to recovery, just halfway between illness and health, that Norah and Max brought the great and unsmiling Von Gerhard on the scene. It appeared that even New York was respectfully aware of Von Gerhard, the nerve specialist, in spite of the fact that he lived in Milwaukee. The idea of bringing him up to look at me occurred to Max quite suddenly. I think it was on the evening that I burst into tears when Max entered the room wearing a squeaky shoe. The Weeping Walrus was a self-contained and tranquil creature compared to me at that time. The sight of a fly on the wall was enough to make me burst into a passion of sobs.

"I know the boy to steady those shaky nerves of yours, Dawn," said Max, after I had made a shamefaced apology for my hysterical weeping, "I'm going to have Von Gerhard up here to look at you. He can run up Sunday, eh, Norah?"

"Who's Von Gerhard?" I inquired, out of the depths of my ignorance. "Anyway, I won't have him. I'll bet he wears a Vandyke and spectacles."

"Von Gerhard!" exclaimed Norah, indignantly. "You ought to be thankful to have him look at you, even if he wears goggles and a flowing beard. Why, even that red-haired New York doctor of yours cringed and looked impressed when I told him that Von Gerhard was a friend of my husband's, and that they had been comrades at Heidelberg. I must have mentioned him dozens of times in my letters."

"Never."

"Queer," commented Max, "he runs up here every now and then to spend a quiet Sunday with Norah and me and the Spalpeens. Says it rests him. The kids swarm all over him, and tear him limb from limb. It doesn't look restful, but he says it's great. I think he came here from Berlin just after you left for New York, Dawn. Milwaukee fits him as if it had been made for him."

"But you're not going to drag this wonderful being up here just for me!" I protested, aghast.

Max pointed an accusing finger at me from the doorway. "Aren't you what the bromides call a bundle of nerves? And isn't Von Gerhard's specialty untying just those knots? I'll write to him to-night."

And he did. And Von Gerhard came. The Spalpeens watched for him, their noses flattened against the window-pane, for it was raining. As he came up the path they burst out of the door to meet him. From my bedroom window I saw him come prancing up the walk like a boy, with the two children clinging to his coat-tails, all three quite unmindful of the rain, and yelling like Comanches.

Ten minutes later he had donned his professional dignity, entered my room, and beheld me in all my limp and pea-green beauty. I noted approvingly that he had to stoop a bit as he entered the low doorway, and that the Vandyke of my prophecy was missing.

He took my hand in his own steady, reassuring clasp. Then he began to talk. Half an hour sped away while we discussed New York—books—music—theatres—everything and anything but Dawn O'Hara. I learned later that as we chatted he was getting his story, bit by bit, from every twitch of the eyelids, from every gesture of the hands that had grown too thin to wear the hateful ring; from every motion of the lips; from the color of my nails; from each convulsive muscle; from every shadow, and wrinkle and curve and line of my face.

Suddenly he asked: "Are you making the proper effort to get well? You try to conquer those jumping nerfs, yes?"

I glared at him. "Try! I do everything. I'd eat woolly worms if I thought they might benefit me. If ever a girl has minded her big sister and her doctor, that girl is I. I've eaten everything from pate de foie gras to raw beef, and I've drunk everything from blood to champagne."

"Eggs?" queried Von Gerhard, as though making a happy suggestion.

"Eggs!" I snorted. "Eggs! Thousands of 'em! Eggs hard and soft boiled, poached and fried, scrambled and shirred, eggs in beer and egg-noggs, egg lemonades and egg orangeades, eggs in wine and eggs in milk, and eggs au naturel. I've lapped up iron-and-wine, and whole rivers of milk, and I've devoured rare porterhouse and roast beef day after day for weeks. So! Eggs!"

"Mein Himmel!" ejaculated he, fervently, "And you still live!" A suspicion of a smile dawned in his eyes. I wondered if he ever laughed. I would experiment.

"Don't breathe it to a soul," I whispered, tragically, "but eggs, and eggs alone, are turning my love for my sister into bitterest hate. She stalks me the whole day long, forcing egg mixtures down my unwilling throat. She bullies me. I daren't put out my hand suddenly without knocking over liquid refreshment in some form, but certainly with an egg lurking in its depths. I am so expert that I can tell an egg orangeade from an egg lemonade at a distance of twenty yards, with my left hand tied behind me, and one eye shut, and my feet in a sack."

"You can laugh, eh? Well, that iss good," commented the grave and unsmiling one.

"Sure," answered I, made more flippant by his solemnity. "Surely I can laugh. For what else was my father Irish? Dad used to say that a sense of humor was like a shillaly—an iligent thing to have around handy, especially when the joke's on you."

The ghost of a twinkle appeared again in the corners of the German blue eyes. Some fiend of rudeness seized me.

"Laugh!" I commanded.

Dr. Ernst von Gerhard stiffened. "Pardon?" inquired he, as one who is sure that he has misunderstood.

"Laugh!" I snapped again. "I'll dare you to do it. I'll double dare you! You dassen't!"

But he did. After a moment's bewildered surprise he threw back his handsome blond head and gave vent to a great, deep infectious roar of mirth that brought the Spalpeens tumbling up the stairs in defiance of their mother's strict instructions.

After that we got along beautifully. He turned out to be quite human, beneath the outer crust of reserve. He continued his examination only after bribing the Spalpeens shamefully, so that even their rapacious demands were satisfied, and they trotted off contentedly.

There followed a process which reduced me to a giggling heap but which Von Gerhard carried out ceremoniously. It consisted of certain raps at my knees, and shins, and elbows, and fingers, and certain commands to—"look at my finger! Look at the wall! Look at my finger! Look at the wall!"

"So!" said Von Gerhard at last, in a tone of finality. I sank my battered frame into the nearest chair. "This—this newspaper work—it must cease." He dismissed it with a wave of the hand.

"Certainly," I said, with elaborate sarcasm. "How should you advise me to earn my living in the future? In the stories they paint dinner cards, don't they? or bake angel cakes?"

"Are you then never serious?" asked Von Gerhard, in disapproval.

"Never," said I. "An old, worn-out, worked-out newspaper reporter, with a husband in the mad-house, can't afford to be serious for a minute, because if she were she'd go mad, too, with the hopelessness of it all." And I buried my face in my hands.

The room was very still for a moment. Then the great Von

Gerhard came over, and took my hands gently from my face. "I—I do beg your pardon," he said. He looked strangely boyish and uncomfortable as he said it. "I was thinking only of your good. We do that, sometimes, forgetting that circumstances may make our wishes impossible of execution. So. You will forgive me?"

"Forgive you? Yes, indeed," I assured him. And we shook hands, gravely. "But that doesn't help matters much, after all, does it?"

"Yes, it helps. For now we understand one another, is it not so? You say you can only write for a living. Then why not write here at home? Surely these years of newspaper work have given you a great knowledge of human nature. Then too, there is your gift of humor. Surely that is a combination which should make your work acceptable to the magazines. Never in my life have I seen so many magazines as here in the United States. But hundreds! Thousands!"

"Me!" I exploded—"A real writer lady! No more interviews with actresses! No more slushy Sunday specials! No more teary tales! Oh, my! When may I begin? To-morrow? You know I brought my typewriter with me. I've almost forgotten where the letters are on the keyboard."

"Wait, wait; not so fast! In a month or two, perhaps. But first must come other things outdoor things. Also housework."

"Housework!" I echoed, feebly.

"Naturlich. A little dusting, a little scrubbing, a little sweeping, a little cooking. The finest kind of indoor exercise. Later you may write a little—but very little. Run and play out of doors with the children. When I see you again you will have roses in your cheeks like the German girls, yes?"

"Yes," I echoed, meekly, "I wonder how Frieda will like my elephantine efforts at assisting with the housework. If she gives notice, Norah will be lost to you."

But Frieda did not give notice. After I had helped her clean the kitchen and the pantry I noticed an expression of deepest pity overspreading her lumpy features. The expression became almost one of agony as she watched me roll out some noodles for soup, and delve into the sticky mysteries of a new kind of cake.

Max says that for a poor working girl who hasn't had time to cultivate the domestic graces, my cakes are a distinct triumph. Sis sniffs at that, and mutters something about cups of raisins and nuts and citron hiding a multitude of batter sins. She never allows the Spalpeens to eat my cakes, and on my baking days they are usually sent from the table howling. Norah declares, severely, that she is going to hide the Green Cook Book. The Green Cook Book is a German one. Norah bought it in deference to Max's love of German cookery. It is called Aunt Julchen's cook book, and the author, between hints as to flour and butter, gets delightfully chummy with her pupil. Her cakes are proud, rich cakes. She orders grandly:

"Now throw in the yolks of twelve eggs; one-fourth of a pound of almonds; two pounds of raisins; a pound of citron; a pound of orange-peel."

As if that were not enough, there follow minor instructions as to trifles like ounces of walnut meats, pounds of confectioner's sugar, and pints of very rich cream. When cold, to be frosted with an icing made up of more eggs, more nuts, more cream, more everything.

The children have appointed themselves official lickers and scrapers of the spoons and icing pans, also official guides on their auntie's walks. They regard their Aunt Dawn as a quite ridiculous but altogether delightful old thing.

And Norah—bless her! looks up when I come in from a romp with the Spalpeens and says: "Your cheeks are pink! Actually! And you're losing a puff there at the back of your ear, and your hat's on crooked. Oh, you are beginning to look your old self, Dawn dear!"

At which doubtful compliment I retort, recklessly: "Pooh! What's a puff more or less, in a worthy cause? And if you think my cheeks are pink now, just wait until your mighty Von Gerhard comes again. By that time they shall be so red and bursting that Frieda's, on wash day, will look anemic by comparison. Say, Norah, how red are German red cheeks, anyway?"

CHAPTER III

GOOD AS NEW

So Spring danced away, and Summer sauntered in. My pillows looked less and less tempting. The wine of the northern air imparted a cocky assurance. One blue-and-gold day followed the other, and I spent hours together out of doors in the sunshine, lying full length on the warm, sweet ground, to the horror of the entire neighborhood. To be sure, I was sufficiently discreet to choose the lawn at the rear of the house. There I drank in the atmosphere, as per doctor's instructions, while the genial sun warmed the watery blood in my veins and burned the skin off the end of my nose.

All my life I had envied the loungers in the parks—those silent, inert figures that lie under the trees all the long summer day, their shabby hats over their faces, their hands clasped above their heads, legs sprawled in uncouth comfort, while the sun dapples down between the leaves and, like a good fairy godmother, touches their frayed and wrinkled garments with flickering figures of golden splendor, while they sleep. They always seemed so blissfully care-free and at ease—those sprawling men figures—and I, to whom such simple joys were forbidden, being a woman, had envied them.

Now I was reveling in that very joy, stretched prone upon the ground, blinking sleepily up at the sun and the cobalt sky, feeling my very hair grow, and health returning in warm, electric waves. I even dared to cross one leg over the other and to swing the pendant member with nonchalant air, first taking a cautious survey of the neighboring back windows to see if any one peeked. Doubtless they did, behind those ruffled curtains, but I grew splendidly indifferent.

Even the crawling things—and there were myriads of them—added to the enjoyment of my ease. With my ear so close to the ground the grass seemed fairly to buzz with them. Everywhere there were crazily busy ants, and I, patently a sluggard and therefore one of those for whom the ancient warning was intended, considered them lazily. How they plunged about, weaving in and out, rushing here and there, helter-skelter, like bargain-hunting women darting wildly from counter to counter!

"O, foolish, foolish antics!" I chided them, "stop wearing yourselves out this way. Don't you know that the game isn't worth the candle, and that you'll give yourselves nervous jim-jams and then you'll have to go home to be patched up? Look at me! I'm a horrible example."

But they only bustled on, heedless of my advice, and showed their contempt by crawling over me as I lay there like a lady Gulliver.

Oh, I played what they call a heavy thinking part. It was not only the ants that came in for lectures. I preached sternly to myself.

"Well, Dawn old girl, you've made a beautiful mess of it. A smashed-up wreck at twenty-eight! And what have you to show for it? Nothing! You're a useless pulp, like a lemon that has been squeezed dry. Von Gerhard was right. There must be no more newspaper work for you, me girl. Not if you can keep away from the fascination of it, which I don't think you can."

Then I would fall to thinking of those years of newspapering—of the thrills of them, and the ills of them. It had been exhilarating, and educating, but scarcely remunerative. Mother had never approved. Dad had chuckled and said that it was a curse descended upon me from the terrible old Kitty O'Hara, the only old maid in the history of the O'Haras, and famed in her day for a caustic tongue and a venomed pen. Dad and Mother—what a pair of children they had been! The very dissimilarity of their natures had been a bond between them. Dad, light-hearted, whimsical, care-free, improvident; Mother, gravely sweet, anxious-browed, trying to teach economy to the handsome Irish husband who, descendant of a long and royal line of spendthrift ancestors, would have none of it.

It was Dad who had insisted that they name me Dawn. Dawn O'Hara! His sense of humor must have been sleeping. "You were such a rosy, pinky, soft baby thing," Mother had once told me, "that you looked just like the first flush of light at sunrise. That is why your father insisted on calling you Dawn."

Poor Dad! How could he know that at twenty-eight I would be a yellow wreck of a newspaper reporter—with a wrinkle between my eyes. If he could see me now he would say:

"Sure, you look like the dawn yet, me girl but a Pittsburgh dawn."

At that, Mother, if she were here, would pat my check where the hollow place is, and murmur: "Never mind, Dawnie dearie, Mother thinks you are beautiful just the same." Of such blessed stuff are mothers made.

At this stage of the memory game I would bury my face in the warm grass and thank my God for having taken Mother before Peter Orme came into my life. And then I would fall asleep there on the soft, sweet grass, with my head snuggled in my arms, and the ants wriggling, unchided, into my ears.

On the last of these sylvan occasions I awoke, not with a graceful start, like the story-book ladies, but with a grunt. Sis was digging me in the ribs with her toe. I looked up to see her standing over me, a foaming tumbler of something in her hand. I felt that it was eggy and eyed it disgustedly.

"Get up," said she, "you lazy scribbler, and drink this."

I sat up, eyeing her severely and picking grass and ants out of my hair.

"D' you mean to tell me that you woke me out of that babe-like slumber to make me drink that goo? What is it, anyway? I'll bet it's another egg-nogg."

"Egg-nogg it is; and swallow it right away, because there are guests to see you."

I emerged from the first dip into the yellow mixture and fixed on her as stern and terrible a look at any one can whose mouth is encircled by a mustache of yellow foam.

"Guests!" I roared, "not for me! Don't you dare to say that they came to see me!"

"Did too," insists Norah, with firmness, "they came especially to see you. Asked for you, right from the jump."

I finished the egg-nogg in four gulps, returned the empty tumbler with an air of decision, and sank upon the grass.

"Tell 'em I rave. Tell 'em that I'm unconscious, and that for weeks I have recognized no one, not even my dear sister. Say that in my present nerve-shattered condition I—"

"That wouldn't satisfy them," Norah calmly interrupts, "they know you're crazy because they saw you out here from their second story back windows. That's why they came. So you may as well get up and face them. I promised them I'd bring you in. You can't go on forever refusing to see people, and you know the Whalens are—"

"Whalens!" I gasped. "How many of them? Not—not the entire fiendish three?"

"All three. I left them champing with impatience."

The Whalens live just around the corner. The Whalens are omniscient. They have a system of news gathering which would make the efforts of a New York daily appear antiquated. They know that Jenny Laffin feeds the family on soup meat and oat-meal when Mr. Laffin is on the road; they know that Mrs. Pearson only shakes out her rugs once in four weeks; they can tell you the number of times a week that Sam Dempster comes home drunk; they know that the Merkles never have cream with their coffee because little Lizzie Merkle goes to the creamery every day with just one pail and three cents; they gloat over the knowledge that Professor Grimes, who is a married man, is sweet on Gertie Ashe, who teaches second reader in his school;

they can tell you where Mrs. Black got her seal coat, and her husband only earning two thousand a year; they know who is going to run for mayor, and how long poor Angela Sims has to live, and what Guy Donnelly said to Min when he asked her to marry him.

The three Whalens—mother and daughters—hunt in a group. They send meaning glances to one another across the room, and at parties they get together and exchange bulletins in a corner. On passing the Whalen house one is uncomfortably aware of shadowy forms lurking in the windows, and of parlor curtains that are agitated for no apparent cause.

Therefore it was with a groan that I rose and prepared to follow Norah into the house. Something in my eye caused her to turn at the very door. "Don't you dare!" she hissed; then, banishing the warning scowl from her face, and assuming a near-smile, she entered the room and I followed miserably at her heels.

The Whalens rose and came forward effusively; Mrs. Whalen, plump, dark, voluble; Sally, lean, swarthy, vindictive; Flossie, pudgy, powdered, over-dressed. They eyed me hungrily. I felt that they were searching my features for signs of incipient insanity.

"Dear, DEAR girl!" bubbled the billowy Flossie, kissing the end of my nose and fastening her eye on my ringless left hand.

Sally contented herself with a limp and fishy handshake. She and I were sworn enemies in our school-girl days, and a baleful gleam still lurked in Sally's eye. Mrs. Whalen bestowed on me a motherly hug that enveloped me in an atmosphere of liquid face-wash, strong perfumery and fried lard. Mrs. Whalen is a famous cook. Said she:

"We've been thinking of calling ever since you were brought home, but dear me! you've been looking so poorly I just said to the girls, wait till the poor thing feels more like seeing her old friends. Tell me, how are you feeling now?"

The three sat forward in their chairs in attitudes of tense waiting.

I resolved that if err I must it should be on the side of safety. I turned to sister Norah.

"How am I feeling anyway, Norah?" I guardedly inquired.

Norah's face was a study. "Why Dawn dear," she said, sugar-sweet, "no doubt you know better than I. But I'm sure that you are wonderfully improved—almost your old self, in fact. Don't you think she looks splendid, Mrs. Whalen?"

The three Whalens tore their gaze from my blank countenance to exchange a series of meaning looks.

"I suppose," purred Mrs. Whalen, "that your awful trouble was the real cause of your—a-a-a-sickness, worrying about it and grieving as you must have."

She pronounces it with a capital T, and I know she means Peter. I hate her for it.

"Trouble!" I chirped. "Trouble never troubles me. I just worked too hard, that's all, and acquired an awful 'tired.' All work and no play makes Jill a nervous wreck, you know."

At that the elephantine Flossie wagged a playful finger at me. "Oh, now, you can't make us believe that, just because we're from the country! We know all about you gay New Yorkers, with your Bohemian ways and your midnight studio suppers, and your cigarettes, and cocktails and high jinks!"

Memory painted a swift mental picture of Dawn O'Hara as she used to tumble into bed after a whirlwind day at the office, too dog-tired to give her hair even one half of the prescribed one hundred strokes of the brush. But in turn I shook a reproving forefinger at Flossie.

"You've been reading some naughty society novel! One of those millionaire-divorce-actress-automobile novels. Dear, dear! Shall I ever forget the first New York actress I ever met; or what she said!"

I felt, more than saw, a warning movement from Sis. But the three Whalens had hitched forward in their chairs.

"What did she say?" gurgled Flossie. "Was it something real reezk?"

"Well, it was at a late supper—a studio supper given in her honor," I confessed.

"Yes-s-s-s," hissed the Whalens.

"And this actress—she was one of those musical comedy actresses, you know; I remember her part called for a good deal of kicking about in a short Dutch costume—came in rather late, after the performance. She was wearing a regal-looking fur-edged evening wrap, and she still wore all her make-up"—out of the corner of my eye I saw Sis sink back with an air of resignation—"and she threw open the door and said—

"Yes-s-s-s!" hissed the Whalens again, wetting their lips.

"—said: 'Folks, I just had a wire from mother, up in Maine. The boy has the croup. I'm scared green. I hate to spoil the party, but don't ask me to stay. I want to go home to the flat and blubber. I didn't even stop to take my make-up off. My God! If anything should happen to the boy!—Well, have a good time without me. Jim's waiting outside.'" A silence.

Then—"Who was Jim?" asked Flossie, hopefully.

"Jim was her husband, of course. He was in the same company."

Another silence.

"Is that all?" demanded Sally from the corner in which she had been glowering.

"All! You unnatural girl! Isn't one husband enough?"

Mrs. Whalen smiled an uncertain, wavering smile. There passed among the three a series of cabalistic signs. They rose simultaneously.

"How quaint you are!" exclaimed Mrs. Whalen, "and so amusing! Come girls, we mustn't tire Miss—ah—Mrs.—er—" with another meaning look at my bare left hand.

"My husband's name is still Orme," I prompted, quite, quite pleasantly.

"Oh, certainly. I'm so forgetful. And one reads such queer things in the newspapers nowa-days. Divorces, and separations, and soul-mates and things." There was a note of gentle insinuation in her voice.

Norah stepped firmly into the fray. "Yes, doesn't one? What a comfort it must be to you to know that your dear girls are safe at home with you, and no doubt will be secure, for years to come, from the buffeting winds of matrimony."

There was a tinge of purple in Mrs. Whalen's face as she moved toward the door, gathering her brood about her. "Now that dear Dawn is almost normal again I shall send my little girlies over real often. She must find it very dull here after her—ah—life in New York."

"Not at all," I said, hurriedly, "not at all. You see I'm—I'm writing a book. My entire day is occupied."

"A book!" screeched the three. "How interesting! What is it? When will it be published?"

I avoided Norah's baleful eye as I answered their questions and performed the final adieux.

As the door closed, Norah and I faced each other, glaring.

"Hussies!" hissed Norah. Whereupon it struck us funny and we fell, a shrieking heap, into the nearest chair. Finally Sis dabbed at her eyes with her handkerchief, drew a long breath, and asked, with elaborate sarcasm, why I hadn't made it a play instead of a book, while I was about it.

"But I mean it," I declared. "I've had enough of loafing. Max must unpack my typewriter to-night. I'm homesick for a look at the keys. And to-morrow I'm to be installed in the cubbyhole off the dining-room and I defy any one to enter it on peril of their lives. If you value the lives of your offspring, warn them away from that door. Von Gerhard said that there was writing in my system, and by the Great Horn Spoon and the Beard of the Prophet, I'll have it out! Besides, I need the money. Norah dear, how does one set about writing a book? It seems like such a large order."

CHAPTER IV

DAWN DEVELOPS A HEIMWEH

It's hard trying to develop into a real Writer Lady in the bosom of one's family, especially when the family refuses to take one seriously. Seven years of newspaper grind have taught me the fallacy of trying to write by the inspiration method. But there is such a thing as a train of thought, and mine is constantly being derailed, and wrecked and pitched about.

Scarcely am I settled in my cubby-hole, typewriter before me, the working plan of a story buzzing about in my brain, when I hear my name called in muffled tones, as though the speaker were laboring with a mouthful of hairpins. I pay no attention. I have just given my heroine a pair of calm gray eyes, shaded with black lashes and hair to match. A voice floats down from the upstairs regions.

"Dawn! Oh, Dawn! Just run and rescue the cucumbers out of the top of the ice-box, will you? The iceman's coming, and he'll squash 'em."

A parting jab at my heroine's hair and eyes, and I'm off to save the cucumbers.

Back at my typewriter once more. Shall I make my heroine petite or grande? I decide that stateliness and Gibsonesque height should accompany the calm gray eyes. I rattle away happily, the plot unfolding itself in some mysterious way. Sis opens the door a little and peers in. She is dressed for the street.

"Dawn dear, I'm going to the dressmaker's. Frieda's upstairs cleaning the bathroom, so take a little squint at the roast now and then, will you? See that it doesn't burn, and that there's plenty of gravy. Oh, and Dawn—tell the milkman we want an extra half-pint of cream to-day. The tickets are on the kitchen shelf, back of the clock. I'll be back in an hour."

"Mhmph," I reply.

Sis shuts the door, but opens it again almost immediately.

"Don't let the Infants bother you. But if Frieda's upstairs and they come to you for something to eat, don't let them have any cookies before dinner. If they're really hungry they'll eat bread and butter."

I promise, dreamily, my last typewritten sentence still running through my head. The gravy seems to have got into the heroine's calm gray eyes. What heroine could remain calm-eyed when her creator's mind is filled with roast beef? A half-hour elapses before I get back on the track. Then appears the hero—a tall blond youth, fair to behold. I make him two yards high, and endow him with a pair of clothing-advertisement shoulders.

There assails my nostrils a fearful smell of scorching. The roast! A wild rush into the kitchen. I fling open the oven door. The roast is mahogany-colored, and gravyless. It takes fifteen minutes of the most desperate first-aid-to-the-injured measures before the roast is revived.

Back to the writing. It has lost its charm. The gray-eyed heroine is a stick; she moves like an Indian lady outside a cigar shop. The hero is a milk-and-water sissy, without a vital spark in him. What's the use of trying to write, anyway? Nobody wants my stuff. Good for nothing except dubbing on a newspaper!

Rap! Rap! Rappity-rap-rap! Bing! Milk!

I dash into the kitchen. No milk! No milkman! I fly to the door. He is disappearing around the corner of the house.

"Hi! Mr. Milkman! Say, Mr. Milkman!" with frantic beckonings.

He turns. He lifts up his voice. "The screen door was locked so I left youse yer milk on top of the ice-box on the back porch. Thought like the hired girl was upstairs an' I could git the tickets to-morra."

I explain about the cream, adding that it is wanted for short-cake. The explanation does not seem to cheer him. He appears to be a very gloomy and reserved milkman. I fancy that he is in the habit of indulging in a little airy persiflage with Frieda o' mornings, and he finds me a poor substitute for her red-cheeked comeliness.

The milk safely stowed away in the ice-box, I have another look at the roast. I am dipping up spoonfuls of brown gravy and pouring them over the surface of the roast in approved basting style, when there is a rush, a scramble, and two hard bodies precipitate themselves upon my legs so suddenly that for a moment my head pitches forward into the oven. I withdraw my head from the oven, hastily. The basting spoon is immersed in the bottom of the pan. I turn, indignant. The Spalpeens look up at me with innocent eyes.

"You little divils, what do you mean by shoving your old aunt into the oven! It's cannibals you are!"

The idea pleases them. They release my legs and execute a savage war dance around me. The Spalpeens are firm in the belief that I was brought to their home for their sole amusement, and they refuse to take me seriously. The Spalpeens themselves are two of the finest examples of real humor that ever were perpetrated upon parents. Sheila is the first-born. Norah decided that she should be an Irish beauty, and bestowed upon her a name that reeks of the bogs. Whereupon Sheila, at the age of six, is as flaxen-haired and blue-eyed and stolid a little German madchen as ever fooled her parents, and she is a feminine reproduction of her German Dad. Two years later came a sturdy boy, and they named him Hans, in a flaunt of defiance. Hans is black-haired, gray-eyed and Irish as Killarny.

"We're awful hungry," announces Sheila.

"Can't you wait until dinner time? Such a grand dinner!"

Sheila and Hans roll their eyes to convey to me that, were they to wait until dinner for sustenance we should find but their lifeless forms.

"Well then, Auntie will get a nice piece of bread and butter for each of you."

"Don't want bread an' butty!" shrieks Hans. "Want tooky!"

"Cooky!" echoes Sheila, pounding on the kitchen table with the rescued basting spoon.

"You can't have cookies before dinner. They're bad for your insides."

"Can too," disputes Hans. "Fwieda dives us tookies. Want tooky!" wailingly.

"Please, ple-e-e-ease, Auntie Dawnie dearie," wheedles Sheila, wriggling her soft little fingers in my hand.

"But Mother never lets you have cookies before dinner," I retort severely. "She knows they are bad for you."

"Pooh, she does too! She always says, 'No, not a cooky!' And then we beg and screech, and then she says, 'Oh, for pity's sake, Frieda, give 'em a cooky and send 'em out. One cooky can't kill 'em.'" Sheila's imitation is delicious.

Hans catches the word screech and takes it as his cue. He begins a series of ear-piercing wails. Sheila surveys him with pride and then takes the wail up in a minor key. Their teamwork is marvelous. I fly to the cooky jar and extract two round and sugary confections. I thrust them into the pink, eager palms. The wails cease. Solemnly they place one cooky atop the other, measuring the circlets with grave eyes.

"Mine's a weeny bit bigger'n yours this time," decides Sheila, and holds her cooky heroically while Hans takes a just and lawful bite out of his sister's larger share.

"The blessed little angels!" I say to myself, melting. "The dear, unselfish little sweeties!" and give each of them another cooky.

Back to my typewriter. But the words flatly refuse to come now. I make six false starts, bite all my best finger-nails, screw my hair into a wilderness of cork-screws and give it up. No doubt a real Lady Writer could write on, unruffled and unhearing, while the iceman squashed the cucumbers, and the roast burned to a frazzle, and the Spalpeens perished of hunger. Possessed of the real spark of genius, trivialities like milkmen and cucumbers could not dim its glow. Perhaps all successful Lady Writers with real live sparks have cooks and scullery maids, and need not worry about basting, and gravy, and milkmen.

This book writing is all very well for those who have a large faith in the future and an equally large bank account. But my future will have to be hand-carved, and my bank account has always been an all too small pay envelope at the end of each week. It will be months before the book is shaped and finished. And my pocketbook is empty. Last week Max sent money for the care of Peter. He and Norah think that I do not know.

Von Gerhard was here in August. I told him that all my firm resolutions to forsake newspaperdom forever were slipping away, one by one.

"I have heard of the fascination of the newspaper office," he said, in his understanding way. "I believe you have a heimweh for it, not?"

"Heimweh! That's the word," I had agreed. "After you have been a newspaper writer for seven years—and loved it—you will be a newspaper writer, at heart and by instinct at least, until you die. There's no getting away from it. It's in the blood. Newspaper men have been known to inherit fortunes, to enter politics, to write books and become famous, to degenerate into press agents and become infamous, to blossom into personages, to sink into nonentities, but their news-nose remained a part of them, and the inky, smoky, stuffy smell of a newspaper office was ever sweet in their nostrils."

But, "Not yet," Von Gerhard had said, "It unless you want to have again this miserable business of the sick nerfs. Wait yet a few months."

And so I have waited, saying nothing to Norah and Max. But I want to be in the midst of things. I miss the sensation of having my fingers at the pulse of the big old world. I'm lonely for the noise and the rush and the hard work; for a glimpse of the busy local room just before press time, when the lights are swimming in a smoky haze, and the big presses downstairs are thundering their warning to hurry, and the men are breezing in from their runs with the grist of news that will be ground finer and finer as it passes through the mill of copy-readers' and editors' hands. I want to be there in the thick of the confusion that is, after all, so orderly. I want to be there when the telephone bells are zinging, and the typewriters are snapping, and the messenger boys are shuffling in and out, and the office kids are scuffling in a corner, and the big city editor, collar off, sleeves rolled up from his great arms, hair bristling wildly above his green eye-shade, is swearing gently and smoking cigarette after cigarette, lighting each fresh one at the dying glow of the last. I would give a year of my life to hear him say:

"I don't mind tellin' you, Beatrice Fairfax, that that was a darn good story you got on the Millhaupt divorce. The other fellows haven't a word that isn't re-hash."

All of which is most unwomanly; for is not marriage woman's highest aim, and home her true sphere? Haven't I tried both? I ought to know. I merely have been miscast in this life's drama. My part should have been that of one who makes her way alone. Peter, with his thin, cruel lips, and his shaking hands, and his haggard face and his smoldering eyes, is a shadow forever blotting out the sunny places in my path. I was meant to be an old maid, like the terrible old Kitty O'Hara. Not one of the tatting-and-tea kind, but an impressive, bustling old girl, with a double chin. The sharp-tongued Kitty O'Hara used to say that being an old maid was a great deal like death by drowning—a really delightful sensation when you ceased struggling.

Norah has pleaded with me to be more like other women of my age, and for her sake I've tried. She has led me about to bridge parties and tea fights, and I have tried to act as though I were enjoying it all, but I knew that I wasn't getting on a bit. I have come to the conclusion that one year of newspapering counts for two years of ordinary, existence, and that while I'm twenty-eight in the family Bible I'm fully forty inside. When one day may bring under one's pen a priest, a pauper, a prostitute, a philanthropist, each with a story to tell, and each requiring to be bullied, or cajoled, or bribed, or threatened, or tricked into telling it; then the end of that day's work finds one looking out at the world with eyes that are very tired and as old as the world itself.

I'm spoiled for sewing bees and church sociables and afternoon bridges. A hunger for the city is upon me. The long, lazy summer days have slipped by. There is an autumn tang in the air. The breeze has a touch that is sharp.

Winter in a little northern town! I should go mad. But winter in the city! The streets at dusk on a frosty evening; the shop windows arranged by artist hands for the beauty-loving eyes of women; the rows of lights like jewels strung on an invisible chain; the glitter of brass and enamel as the endless procession of motors flashes past; the smartly-gowned women; the keen-eyed, nervous men; the shrill note of the crossing policeman's whistle; every smoke-grimed wall and pillar taking on a mysterious shadowy beauty in the purple dusk, every unsightly blot obscured by the kindly night. But best of all, the fascination of the People I'd Like to Know. They pop up now and then in the shifting crowds, and are gone the next moment, leaving behind them a vague regret. Sometimes I call them the People I'd Like to Know and sometimes I call them the People I Know I'd Like, but it means much the same. Their faces flash by in the crowd, and are gone, but I recognize them instantly as belonging to my beloved circle of unknown friends.

Once it was a girl opposite me in a car—a girl with a wide, humorous mouth, and tragic eyes, and a hole in her shoe. Once it was a big, homely, red-headed giant of a man with an engineering magazine sticking out of his coat pocket. He was standing at a book counter reading Dickens like a schoolboy and laughing in all the right places, I know, because I peaked over his shoulder to see. Another time it was a sprightly little, grizzled old woman, staring into a dazzling shop window in which was displayed a wonderful collection of fashionably impossible hats and gowns. She was dressed all in rusty black, was the little old lady, and she had a quaint cast in her left eye that gave her the oddest, most sporting look. The cast was working overtime as she gazed at the gowns, and the ridiculous old sprigs on her rusty black bonnet trembled with her silent mirth. She looked like one of those clever, epigrammatic, dowdy old duchesses that one reads about in English novels. I'm sure she had cardamon seeds in her shabby bag, and a carriage with a crest on it waiting for her just around the corner. I ached to slip my hand through her arm and ask her what she thought of it all. I know that her reply would have been exquisitely witty and audacious, and I did so long to hear her say it.

No doubt some good angel tugs at my common sense, restraining me from doing these things that I am tempted to do. Of course it would be madness for a woman to address unknown red-headed men with the look of an engineer about them and a book of Dickens in their hands; or perky old women with nutcracker faces; or girls with wide humorous mouths. Oh, it couldn't be done, I suppose. They would clap me in a padded cell in no time if I were to say:

"Mister Red-headed Man, I'm so glad your heart is young enough for Dickens. I love him too—enough to read him standing at a book counter in a busy shop. And do you know, I like the squareness of your jaw, and the way your eyes crinkle up when you laugh; and as for your being an engineer—why one of the very first men I ever loved was the engineer in 'Soldiers of Fortune.'"

I wonder what the girl in the car would have said if I had crossed over to her, and put my hand on her arm and spoken, thus:

"Girl with the wide, humorous mouth, and the tragic eyes, and the hole in your shoe, I think you must be an awfully good sort. I'll wager you paint, or write, or act, or do something clever like that for a living. But from that hole in your shoe which you have inked so carefully, although it persists in showing white at the seams, I fancy you are stumbling over a rather stony bit of Life's road just now. And from the look in your eyes, girl, I'm afraid the stones have cut and bruised rather cruelly. But when I look at your smiling, humorous mouth I know that you are trying to laugh at the hurts. I think that this morning, when you inked your shoe for the dozenth time, you hesitated between tears and laughter, and the laugh won, thank God! Please keep right on laughing, and don't you dare stop for a minute! Because pretty soon you'll come to a smooth easy place, and then won't you be glad that you didn't give up to lie down by the roadside, weary of your hurts?"

Oh, it would never do. Never. And yet no charm possessed by the people I know and like can compare with the fascination of those People I'd Like to Know, and Know I Would Like.

Here at home with Norah there are no faces in the crowds. There are no crowds. When you turn the corner at Main street you are quite sure that you will see the same people in the same places. You know that Mamie Hayes will be flapping her duster just outside the door of the jewelry store where she clerks. She gazes up and down Main street as she flaps the cloth, her bright eyes keeping a sharp watch for stray traveling men that may chance to be passing. You know that there will be the same lounging group of white-faced, vacant-eyed youths outside the pool-room. Dr. Briggs's patient runabout will be standing at his office doorway. Outside his butcher shop Assemblyman Schenck will be holding forth on the subject of county politics to a group of red-faced, badly dressed, prosperous looking farmers and townsmen, and as he talks the circle of brown tobacco juice which surrounds the group closes in upon them, nearer and nearer. And there, in a roomy chair in a corner of the public library reference room, facing the big front window, you will see Old Man Randall. His white hair forms a halo above his pitiful drink-marred face. He was to have been a great lawyer, was Old Man Randall. But on the road to fame he met Drink, and she grasped his arm, and led him down by-ways, and into crooked lanes, and finally into ditches, and he never arrived at his goal. There in that library window nook it is cool in summer, and warm in winter. So he sits and dreams, holding an open volume, unread, on his knees. Some times he writes, hunched up in his corner, feverishly scribbling at ridiculous plays, short stories, and novels which later he will insist on reading to the tittering schoolboys and girls who come into the library to do their courting and reference work. Presently, when it grows dusk, Old Man Randall will put away his book, throw his coat over his shoulders, sleeves dangling, flowing white locks sweeping the frayed velvet collar. He will march out with his soldierly tread, humming a bit of a tune, down the street and into Vandermeister's saloon, where he will beg a drink and a lunch, and some man will give it to him for the sake of what Old Man Randall might have been.

All these things you know. And knowing them, what is left for the imagination? How can one dream dreams about people when one knows how much they pay their hired girl, and what they have for dinner on Wednesdays?

CHAPTER V

THE ABSURD BECOMES SERIOUS

I can understand the emotions of a broken-down war horse that is hitched to a vegetable wagon. I am going to Milwaukee to work! It is a thing to make the gods hold their sides and roll down from their mountain peaks with laughter. After New York—Milwaukee!

Of course Von Gerhard is to blame. But I think even he sees the humor of it. It happened in this way, on a day when I was indulging in a particularly greenery-yallery fit of gloom. Norah rushed into my room. I think I was mooning over some old papers, or letters, or ribbons, or some such truck in the charming, knife-turning way that women have when they are blue.

"Out wid yez!" cried Norah. "On with your hat and coat! I've just had a wire from Ernst von Gerhard. He's coming, and you look like an under-done dill pickle. You aren't half as blooming as when he was here in August, and this is October. Get out and walk until your cheeks are so red that Von Gerhard will refuse to believe that this fiery-faced puffing, bouncing creature is the green and limp thing that huddled in a chair a few months ago. Out ye go!"

And out I went. Hatless, I strode countrywards, leaving paved streets and concrete walks far behind. There were drifts of fallen leaves all about, and I scuffled through them drearily, trying to feel gloomy, and old, and useless, and failing because of the tang in the air, and the red-and-gold wonder of the frost-kissed leaves, and the regular pump-pump of good red blood that was coursing through my body as per Norah's request.

In a field at the edge of the town, just where city and country begin to have a bowing acquaintance, the college boys were at football practice. Their scarlet sweaters made gay patches of color against the dull gray-brown of the autumn grass.

"Seven-eighteen-two-four!" called a voice. There followed a scuffle, a creaking of leather on leather, a thud. I watched them, a bit enviously, walking backwards until a twist in the road hid them from view. That same twist transformed my path into a real country road—a brown, dusty, monotonous Michigan country road that went severely about its business, never once stopping to flirt with the blushing autumn woodland at its left, or to dally with the dimpling ravine at its right.

"Now if that were an English country road," thought I, "a sociably inclined, happy-go-lucky, out-for-pleasure English country road, one might expect something of it. On an English country road this would be the psychological moment for the appearance of a blond god, in gray tweed. What a delightful time of it Richard Le Gallienne's hero had on his quest! He could not stroll down the most innocent looking lane, he might not loiter along the most out-of-the-way path, he never ambled over the barest piece of country road, that he did not come face to face with some witty and lovely woman creature, also in search of things unconventional, and able to quote charming lines from Chaucer to him."

Ah, but that was England, and this is America. I realize it sadly as I step out of the road to allow a yellow milk wagon to rattle past. The red letters on the yellow milk cart inform the reader that it is the property of August Schimmelpfennig, of Hickory Grove. The Schimmelpfennig eye may be seen staring down upon me from the bit of glass in the rear as the cart rattles ahead, doubtless being suspicious of hatless young women wandering along country roads at dusk, alone. There was that in the staring eye to which I took exception. It wore an expression which made me feel sure that the mouth below it was all a-grin, if I could but have seen it. It was bad enough to be stared at by the fishy Schimmelpfennig eye, but to be grinned at by the Schimmelpfennig mouth!—I resented it. In order to show my resentment I turned my back on the Schimmelpfennig cart and pretended to look up the road which I had just traveled.

I pretended to look up the road, and then I did look in earnest. No wonder the Schimmelpfennig eye and mouth had worn the leering expression. The blond god in gray tweed was swinging along toward me! I knew that he was blond because he wore no hat and the last rays of the October sun were making a little halo effect about his head. I knew that his gray clothes were tweed because every well regulated hero on a country road wears tweed. It's almost a religion with them. He was not near enough to make a glance at his features possible. I turned around and continued my walk. The yellow cart, with its impudent Schimmelpfennig leer, was disappearing in a cloud of dust. Shades of the "Duchess" and Bertha M. Clay! How does one greet a blond god in gray tweed on a country road, when one has him!

The blond god solved the problem for me.

"Hi!" he called. I did not turn. There was a moment's silence. Then there came a shrill, insistent whistle, of the kind that is made by placing four fingers between the teeth. It is a favorite with the gallery gods. I would not have believed that gray tweed gods stooped to it.

"Hi!" called the voice again, very near now. "Lieber Gott! Never have I seen so proud a young woman!"

I whirled about to face Von Gerhard; a strangely boyish and unprofessional looking Von Gerhard.

"Young man," I said severely, "have you been a-follerin' of me?"

"For miles," groaned he, as we shook hands. "You walk like a grenadier. I am sent by the charming Norah to tell you that you are to come home to mix the salad dressing, for there is company for supper. I am the company."

I was still a bit dazed. "But how did you know which road to take? And when—"

"Wunderbar, nicht wahr?" laughed Von Gerhard. "But really quite simple. I come in on an earlier train than I had expected, chat a moment with sister Norah, inquire after the health of my patient, and am told that she is running away from a horde of blue devils!—quote your charming sister—that have swarmed about her all day. What direction did her flight take? I ask. Sister Norah shrugs her shoulders and presumes that it is the road which shows the reddest and yellowest autumn colors. That road will be your road. So!"

"Pooh! How simple! That is the second disappointment you have given me to-day."

"But how is that possible? The first has not had time to happen."

"The first was yourself," I replied, rudely.

"I had been longing for an adventure. And when I saw you 'way up the road, such an unusual figure for our Michigan country roads, I forgot that I was a disappointed old grass widder with a history, and I grew young again, and my heart jumped up into my throat, and I sez to mesilf, sez I: 'Enter the hero!' And it was only you."

Von Gerhard stared a moment, a curious look on his face. Then he laughed one of those rare laughs of his, and I joined him because I was strangely young, light, and happy to be alive.

"You walk and enjoy walking, yes?" asked Von Gerhard, scanning my face. "Your cheeks they are like—well, as unlike the cheeks of the German girls as Diana's are unlike a dairy maid's. And the nerfs? They no longer jump, eh?"

"Oh, they jump, but not with weariness. They jump to get into action again. From a life of too much excitement I have gone to the other extreme. I shall be dead of ennui in another six months."

"Ennui?" mused he, "and you are—how is it?—twenty-eight years, yes? H'm!"

There was a world of exasperation in the last exclamation.

"I am a thousand years old," it made me exclaim, "a million!"

"I will prove to you that you are sixteen," declared Von

Gerhard, calmly.

We had come to a fork in the road. At the right the narrower road ran between two rows of great maples that made an arch of golden splendor. The frost had kissed them into a gorgeous radiance.

"Sunshine Avenue," announced Von Gerhard. "It beckons us away from home, and supper and salad dressing and duty, but who knows what we shall find at the end of it!"

"Let's explore," I suggested. "It is splendidly golden enough to be enchanted."

We entered the yellow canopied pathway.

"Let us pretend this is Germany, yes?" pleaded Von Gerhard. "This golden pathway will end in a neat little glass-roofed restaurant, with tables and chairs outside, and comfortable German papas and mammas and pig-tailed children sitting at the tables, drinking coffee or beer. There will be stout waiters, and a red-faced host. And we will seat ourselves at one of the tables, and I will wave my hand, and one of the stout waiters will come flying. 'Will you have coffee, *Fraulein*, or beer?' It sounds prosaic, but it is very, very good, as you will see. Pathways in Germany always end in coffee and Kuchen and waiters in white aprons."

But, "Oh, no!" I exclaimed, for his mood was infectious. "This is France. Please! The golden pathway will end in a picturesque little French farm, with a dairy. And in the doorway of the farmhouse there will be a red-skirted peasant woman, with a white cap! and a baby on her arm! and sabots! Oh, surely she will wear sabots!"

"Most certainly she will wear sabots," Von Gerhard said, heatedly, "and blue knitted stockings. And the baby's name is Mimi!"

We had taken hands and were skipping down the pathway now, like two excited children.

"Let's run," I suggested. And run we did, like two mad creatures, until we rounded a gentle curve and brought up, panting, within a foot of a decrepit rail fence. The rail fence enclosed a stubbly, lumpy field. The field was inhabited by an inquiring cow. Von Gerhard and I stood quite still, hand in hand, gazing at the cow. Then we turned slowly and looked at each other.

"This pathway of glorified maples ends in a cow," I said, solemnly. At which we both shrieked with mirth, leaning on the decrepit fence and mopping our eyes with our handkerchiefs.

"Did I not say you were sixteen?" taunted Von Gerhard. We were getting surprisingly well acquainted.

"Such a scolding as we shall get! It will be quite dark before we are home. Norah will be tearing her hair."

It was a true prophecy. As we stampeded up the steps the door was flung open, disclosing a tragic figure.

"Such a steak!" wailed Norah, "and it has been done for hours and hours, and now it looks like a piece of fried ear. Where have you two driveling idiots been? And mushrooms too."

"She means that the ruined steak was further enhanced by mushrooms," I explained in response to Von Gerhard's bewildered look. We marched into the house, trying not to appear like sneak thieves. Max, pipe in mouth, surveyed us blandly.

"Fine color you've got, Dawn," he remarked.

"There is such a thing as overdoing this health business," snapped Norah, with a great deal of acidity for her. "I didn't tell you to make them purple, you know."

Max turned to Von Gerhard. "Now what does she mean by that do you suppose, eh Ernst?"

"Softly, brother, softly!" whispered Von Gerhard. "When women exchange remarks that apparently are simple, and yet that you, a man, cannot understand, then know there is a woman's war going on, and step softly, and hold your peace. Aber ruhig!"

Calm was restored with the appearance of the steak, which was found to have survived the period of waiting, and to be incredibly juicy and tender. Presently we were all settled once more in the great beamed living room, Sis at the piano, the two men smoking their after-dinner cigars with that idiotic expression of contentment which always adorns the masculine face on such occasions.

I looked at them—at those three who had done so much for my happiness and well being, and something within me said: "Now! Speak now!" Norah was playing very softly, so that the Spalpeens upstairs might not be disturbed. I took a long breath and made the plunge.

"Norah, if you'll continue the slow music, I'll be much obliged. 'The time has come, the Walrus said, to talk of many things.'"

"Don't be absurd," said Norah, over her shoulder, and went on playing.

"I never was more serious in my life, good folkses all. I've got to be. This butterfly existence has gone on long enough. Norah, and Max, and Mr. Doctor Man, I am going away."

Norah's hands crashed down on the piano keys with a jangling discord. She swung about to face me.

"Not New York again, Dawn! Not New York!"

"I am afraid so," I answered.

Max—bless his great, brotherly heart—rose and came over to me and put a hand on my shoulder.

"Don't you like it here, girlie? Want to be hauled home on a shutter again, do you? You know that as long as we have a home, you have one. We need you here."

But I shook my head. From his chair at the other side of the room I could feel Von Gerhard's gaze fixed upon us. He had said nothing.

"Need me! No one needs me. Don't worry; I'm not going to become maudlin about it. But I don't belong here, and you know, it. I have my work to do. Norah is the best sister that a woman ever had. And Max, you're an angel brother-in-law. But how can I stay on here and keep my self-respect?" I took Max's big hand in mine and gathered courage from it.

"But you have been working," wailed Norah, "every morning.

And I thought the book was coming on beautifully. And I'm sure it will be a wonderful book, Dawn dear. You are so clever."

"Oh, the book—it is too uncertain. Perhaps it will go, but perhaps it won't. And then—what? It will be months before the book is properly polished off. And then I may peddle it around for more months. No; I can't afford to trifle with uncertainties. Every newspaper man or woman writes a book. It's like having the measles. There is not a newspaper man living who does not believe, in his heart, that if he could only take a month or two away from the telegraph desk or the police run, he could write the book of the year, not to speak of the great American Play. Why, just look at me! I've only been writing seriously for a few weeks, and already the best magazines in the country are refusing my manuscripts daily."

"Don't joke," said Norah, coming over to me, "I can't stand it."

"Why not? Much better than weeping, isn't it? And anyway, I'm no subject for tears any more. Dr. von Gerhard will tell you how well and strong I am. Won't you, Herr Doktor?"

"Well," said Von Gerhard, in his careful, deliberate English, "since you ask me, I should say that you might last about one year, in New York."

"There! What did I tell you!" cried Norah.

"What utter blither!" I scoffed, turning to glare at Von Gerhard.

"Gently," warned Max. "Such disrespect to the man who pulled you back from the edge of the yawning grave only six months ago!"

"Yawning fiddlesticks!" snapped I, elegantly. "There was nothing wrong with me except that I wanted to be fussed over. And I have been. And I've loved it. But it must stop now." I rose and walked over to the table and faced Von Gerhard, sitting there in the depths of a great chair. "You do not seem to realize that I am not free to come and go, and work and play, and laugh and live like other women. There is my living to make. And there is—Peter Orme. Do you think that I could stay on here like this?

Oh, I know that Max is not a poor man. But he is not a rich man, either. And there are the children to be educated, and besides, Max married Norah O'Hara, not the whole O'Hara tribe. I want to go to work. I am not a free woman, but when I am working, I forget, and am almost happy. I tell you I must be well again! I will be well! I am well!"

At the end of which dramatic period I spoiled the whole effect by bowing my head on the table and giving way to a fit of weeping such as I had not had since the days of my illness.

"Looks like it," said Max, at which I decided to laugh, and the situation was saved.

It was then that Von Gerhard proposed the thing that set us staring at him in amused wonder. He came over and stood looking down at us, his hands outspread upon the big library table, his body bent forward in an attitude of eager intentness. I remember thinking what wonderful hands they were, true indexes of the man's character; broad, white, surgeonly hands; the fingers almost square at the tips. They were hands as different from those slender, nervous, unsteady, womanly hands of Peter Orme as any hands could be, I thought. They were hands made for work that called for delicate strength, if such a paradox could be; hands to cling to; to gain courage from; hands that spelled power and reserve. I looked at them, fascinated, as I often had done before, and thought that I never had seen such SANE hands.

"You have done me the honor to include me in this little family conclave," began Ernst von Gerhard. "I am going to take advantage of your trust. I shall give you some advice—a thing I usually keep for unpleasant professional occasions. Do not go back to New York."

"But I know New York. And New York—the newspaper part of it—knows me. Where else can I go?"

"You have your book to finish. You could never finish it there, is it not so?"

I'm afraid I shrugged my shoulders. It was all so much harder than I had expected. What did they want me to do? I asked myself, bitterly.

Von Gerhard went on. "Why not go where the newspaper work will not be so nerve-racking? where you still might find time for this other work that is dear to you, and that may bring its reward in time." He reached out and took my hand, into his great, steady clasp. "Come to the happy, healthy, German town called Milwaukee, yes? Ach, you may laugh. But newspaper work is newspaper work the world over, because men and women are just men and women the world over. But there you could live sanely, and work not too hard, and there would be spare hours for the book that is near your heart. And I—I will speak of you to Norberg, of the Post. And on Sundays, if you are good, I may take you along the marvelous lake drives in my little red runabout, yes? Aber wunderbar, those drives are! So."

Then—"Milwaukee!" shrieked Max and Norah and I, together. "After New York—Milwaukee!"

"Laugh," said Von Gerhard, quite composedly. "I give you until to-morrow morning to stop laughing. At the end of that time it will not seem quite so amusing. No joke is so funny after one has contemplated it for twelve hours."

The voice of Norah, the temptress, sounded close to my ear. "Dawn dear, just think how many million miles nearer you would be to Max, and me, and home."

"Oh, you have all gone mad! The thing is impossible. I shan't go back to a country sheet in my old age. I suppose that in two more years I shall be editing a mothers' column on an agricultural weekly."

"Norberg would be delighted to get you," mused Von Gerhard, "and it would be day work instead of night work."

"And you would send me a weekly bulletin on Dawn's health, wouldn't you, Ernst?" pleaded Norah. "And you'd teach her to drink beer and she shall grow so fat that the Spalpeens won't know their auntie."

At last—"How much do they pay?" I asked, in desperation.

And the thing that had appeared so absurd at first began to take on the shape of reality.

Von Gerhard did speak to Norberg of the Post. And I am to go to Milwaukee next week. The skeleton of the book manuscript is stowed safely away in the bottom of my trunk and Norah has filled in the remaining space with sundry flannels, and hot water bags and medicine flasks, so that I feel like a schoolgirl on her way to boarding-school, instead of like a seasoned old newspaper woman with a capital PAST and a shaky future. I wish that I were chummier with the Irish saints. I need them now.

CHAPTER VI

STEEPED IN GERMAN

I am living at a little private hotel just across from the court house square with its scarlet geraniums and its pretty fountain. The house is filled with German civil engineers, mechanical engineers, and Herr Professors from the German academy. On Sunday mornings we have Pfannkuchen with currant jelly, and the Herr Professors come down to breakfast in fearful flappy German slippers. I'm the only creature in the place that isn't just over from Germany. Even the dog is a dachshund. It is so unbelievable that every day or two I go down to Wisconsin Street and gaze at the stars and stripes floating from the government building, in order to convince myself that this is America. It needs only a Kaiser or so, and a bit of Unter den Linden to be quite complete.

The little private hotel is kept by Herr and Frau Knapf. After one has seen them, one quite understands why the place is steeped in a German atmosphere up to its eyebrows.

I never would have found it myself. It was Doctor von Gerhard who had suggested Knapf's, and who had paved the way for my coming here.

"You will find it quite unlike anything you have ever tried before," he warned me. "Very German it is, and very, very clean, and most inexpensive. Also I think you will find material there—how is it you call it?—copy, yes? Well, there should be copy in plenty; and types! But you shall see."

From the moment I rang the Knapf doorbell I saw. The dapper, cheerful Herr Knapf, wearing a disappointed Kaiser

Wilhelm mustache, opened the door. I scarcely had begun to make my wishes known when he interrupted with a large wave of the hand, and an elaborate German bow.

"Ach yes! You would be the lady of whom the Herr Doktor has spoken. Gewiss! Frau Orme, not? But so a young lady I did not expect to see. A room we have saved for you—aber wunderhubsch! It makes me much pleasure to show. Folgen Sie mir, bitte."

"You—you speak English?" I faltered, with visions of my evenings spent in expressing myself in the sign language.

"Englisch? But yes. Here in Milwaukee it gives aber mostly German. And then too, I have been only twenty years in this country. And always in Milwaukee. Here is it gemutlich—and mostly it gives German."

I tried not to look frightened, and followed him up to the "but wonderfully beautiful" room. To my joy I found it high-ceilinged, airy, and huge, with a great vault of a clothes closet bristling with hooks, and boasting an unbelievable number of shelves. My trunk was swallowed up in it. Never in all my boarding-house experience have I seen such a room, or such a closet. The closet must have been built for a bride's trousseau in the days of hoop-skirts and scuttle bonnets. There was a separate and distinct hook for each and every one of my most obscure garments. I tried to spread them out. I used two hooks to every petticoat, and three for my kimono, and when I had finished there were rows of hooks to spare. Tiers of shelves yawned for hat-boxes which I possessed not. Bluebeard's wives could have held a family reunion in that closet and invited all of Solomon's spouses. Finally, in desperation, I gathered all my poor garments together and hung them in a sociable bunch on the hooks nearest the door. How I should have loved to have shown that closet to a select circle of New York boarding-house landladies!

After wrestling in vain with the forest of hooks, I turned my attention to my room. I yanked a towel thing off the center table and replaced it with a scarf that Peter had picked up in the Orient. I set up my typewriter in a corner near a window and dug a gay cushion or two and a chafing-dish out of my trunk. I distributed photographs of Norah and Max and the Spalpeens separately, in couples, and in groups. Then I bounced up and down in a huge yellow brocade chair and found it unbelievably soft and comfortable. Of course, I reflected, after the big veranda, and the apple tree at Norah's, and the leather-cushioned comfort of her library, and the charming tones of her Oriental rugs and hangings—

"Oh, stop your carping, Dawn!" I told myself. "You can't expect charming tones, and Oriental do-dads and apple trees in a German boarding-house. Anyhow there's running water in the room. For general utility purposes that's better than a pink prayer rug."

There was a time when I thought that it was the luxuries that made life worth living. That was in the old Bohemian days.

"Necessities!" I used to laugh, "Pooh! Who cares about the necessities! What if the dishpan does leak? It is the luxuries that count."

Bohemia and luxuries! Half a dozen lean boarding-house years have steered me safely past that. After such a course in common sense you don't stand back and examine the pictures of a pink Moses in a nest of purple bullrushes, or complain because the bureau does not harmonize with the wall paper. Neither do you criticize the blue and saffron roses that form the rug pattern. 'Deedy not! Instead you warily punch the mattress to see if it is rock-stuffed, and you snoop into the clothes closet; you inquire the distance to the nearest bath room, and whether the payments are weekly or monthly, and if there is a baby in the room next door. Oh, there's nothing like living in a boarding-house for cultivating the materialistic side.

But I was to find that here at Knapf's things were quite different. Not only was Ernst von Gerhard right in saying that it was "very German, and very, very clean;" he recognized good copy when he saw it. Types! I never dreamed that such faces existed outside of the old German woodcuts that one sees illustrating time-yellowed books.

I had thought myself hardened to strange boarding-house dining rooms, with their batteries of cold, critical women's eyes. I had learned to walk unruffled in the face of the most carping, suspicious and the fishiest of these batteries. Therefore on my first day at Knapf's I went down to dinner in the evening, quite composed and secure in the knowledge that my collar was clean and that there was no flaw to find in the fit of my skirt in the back.

As I opened the door of my room I heard sounds as of a violent altercation in progress downstairs. I leaned over the balusters and listened. The sounds rose and fell and swelled and boomed. They were German sounds that started in the throat, gutturally, and spluttered their way up. They were sounds such as I had not heard since the night I was sent to cover a Socialist meeting in New York. I tip-toed down the stairs, although I might have fallen down and landed with a thud without having been heard. The din came from the direction of the dining room. Well, come what might, I would not falter. After all, it could not be worse than that awful time when I had helped cover the teamsters' strike. I peered into the dining room.

The thunder of conversation went on as before. But there was no bloodshed. Nothing but men and women sitting at small tables, eating and talking. When I say eating and talking I do not mean that those acts were carried on separately. Not at all. The eating and the talking went on simultaneously, neither interrupting the other. A fork full of food and a mouthful of ten-syllabled German words met, wrestled, and passed one another, unscathed. I stood in the doorway, fascinated, until Herr Knapf spied me, took a nimble skip in my direction, twisted the discouraged mustaches into temporary sprightliness, and waved me toward a table in the center of the room.

Then a frightful thing happened. When I think of it now I turn cold. The battery was not that of women's eyes, but of men's. And conversation ceased! The uproar and the booming of vowels was hushed. The silence was appalling. I looked up in horror to find that what seemed to be millions of staring blue eyes were fixed on me. The stillness was so thick that you could cut it with a knife. Such men! Immediately I dubbed them the aborigines, and prayed that I might find adjectives with which to describe their foreheads.

It appeared that the aborigines were especially favored in that they were all placed at one long, untidy table at the head of the room. The rest of us sat at small tables. Later I learned that they were all engineers. At meals they discuss engineering problems in the most awe-inspiring German. After supper they smoke impossible German pipes and dozens of cigarettes. They have bulging, knobby foreheads and bristling pompadours, and some of the rawest of them wear wild-looking beards, and thick spectacles, and cravats and trousers that Lew Fields never even dreamed of. They are all graduates of high-sounding foreign universities and are horribly learned and brilliant, but they are the worst mannered lot I ever saw.

In the silence that followed my entrance a red-cheeked maid approached me and asked what I would have for supper. Supper? I asked. Was not dinner served in the evening? The aborigines nudged each other and sniggered like fiendish little school-boys.

The red-cheeked maid looked at me pityingly. Dinner was served in the middle of the day, naturlich. For supper there was Wienerschnitzel, and kalter Aufschnitt, also Kartoffel Salat, and fresh Kaffeekuchen.

The room hung breathless on my decision. I wrestled with a horrible desire to shriek and run. Instead I managed to mumble an order. The aborigines turned to one another inquiringly.

"Was hat sie gesagt?" they asked. "What did she say?" Whereupon they fell to discussing my hair and teeth and eyes and complexion in German as crammed with adjectives as was the rye bread over which I was choking with caraway. The entire table watched me with wide-eyed, unabashed interest while I ate, and I advanced by quick stages from red-faced confusion to purple mirth. It appeared that my presence was the ground for a heavy German joke in connection with the youngest of the aborigines. He was a very plump and greasy looking aborigine with a doll-like rosiness of cheek and a scared and bristling pompadour and very small pig-eyes. The other aborigines clapped him on the back and roared:

"Ai Fritz! Jetzt brauchst du nicht zu weinen! Deine Lena war aber nicht so huebsch, eh?"

Later I learned that Fritz was the newest arrival and that since coming to this country he had been rather low in spirits in consequence of a certain flaxen-haired Lena whom he had left behind in the fatherland.

An examination of the dining room and its other occupants served to keep my mind off the hateful long table. The dining room was a double one, the floor carpetless and clean. There was a little platform at one end with hardy-looking plants in pots near the windows. The wall was ornamented with very German pictures of very plump, bare-armed German girls being chucked under the chin by very dashing, mustachioed German lieutenants. It was all very bare, and strange and foreign to my eyes, and yet there was something bright and comfortable about it. I felt that I was going to like it, aborigines and all. The men drink beer with their supper and read the Staats-Zeitung and the Germania and foreign papers that I never heard of. It is uncanny, in these United States. But it is going to be bully for my German.

After my first letter home Norah wrote frantically, demanding to know if I was the only woman in the house. I calmed her fears by assuring her that, while the men were interesting and ugly with the fascinating ugliness of a bulldog, the women were crushed looking and uninteresting and wore hopeless hats. I have written Norah and Max reams about this household, from the aborigines to Minna, who tidies my room and serves my meals, and admires my clothes. Minna is related to Frau Knapf, whom I have never seen. Minna is inordinately fond of dress, and her remarks anent my own garments are apt to be a trifle disconcerting, especially when she intersperses her recital of dinner dishes with admiring adjectives directed at my blouse or hat. Thus:

"Wir haben roast beef, und spareribs mit Sauerkraut, und schicken—ach, wie schon, Frau Orme! Aber ganz prachtvoll!" Her eyes and hands are raised toward heaven.

"What's prachtful?" I ask, startled. "The chicken?"

"Nein; your waist. Selbst gemacht?"

I am even becoming hardened to the manners of the aborigines. It used to fuss me to death to meet one of them in the halls. They always stopped short, brought heels together with a click, bent stiffly from the waist, and thundered: "Nabben', Fraulein!"

I have learned to take the salutation quite calmly, and even the wildest, most spectacled and knobby-browed aborigine cannot startle me. Nonchalantly I reply, "Nabben'," and wish that Norah could but see me in the act.

When I told Ernst von Gerhard about them, he laughed a little and shrugged his shoulders and said:

"Na, you should not look so young, and so pretty, and so unmarried. In Germany a married woman brushes her hair quite smoothly back, and pins it in a hard knob. And she knows nothing of such bewildering collars and fluffy frilled things in the front of the blouse. How do you call them—jabots?"

Von Gerhard has not behaved at all nicely. I did not see him until two weeks after my arrival in Milwaukee, although he telephoned twice to ask if there was anything that he could do to make me comfortable.

"Yes," I had answered the last time that I heard his voice over the telephone. "It would be a whole heap of comfort to me just to see you. You are the nearest thing to Norah that there is in this whole German town, and goodness knows you're far from Irish."

He came. The weather had turned suddenly cold and he was

wearing a fur-lined coat with a collar of fur. He looked most amazingly handsome and blond and splendidly healthy. The clasp of his hands was just as big and sure as ever.

"You have no idea how glad I am to see you," I told him. "If you had, you would have been here days ago. Aren't you rather ill-mannered and neglectful, considering that you are responsible for my being here?"

"I did not know whether you, a married woman, would care to have me here," he said, in his composed way. "In a place like this people are not always kind enough to take the trouble to understand. And I would not have them raise their eyebrows at you, not for—"

"Married!" I laughed, some imp of willfulness seizing me, "I'm not married. What mockery to say that I am married simply because I must write madam before my name! I am not married, and I shall talk to whom I please."

And then Von Gerhard did a surprising thing. He took two great steps over to my chair, and grasped my hands and pulled me to my feet. I stared up at him like a silly creature. His face was suffused with a dull red, and his eyes were unbelievably blue and bright. He had my hands in his great grip, but his voice was very quiet and contained.

"You are married," he said. "Never forget that for a moment. You are bound, hard and fast and tight. And you are for no man. You are married as much as though that poor creature in the mad house were here working for you, instead of the case being reversed as it is. So."

"What do you mean!" I cried, wrenching myself away indignantly. "What right have you to talk to me like this? You know what my life has been, and how I have tried to smile with my lips and stay young in my heart! I thought you understood. Norah thought so too, and Max—"

"I do understand. I understand so well that I would not have you talk as you did a moment ago. And I said what I said not so much for your sake, as for mine. For see, I too must remember that you write madam before your name. And sometimes it is hard for me to remember."

"Oh," I said, like a simpleton, and stood staring after him as he quietly gathered up his hat and gloves and left me standing there.

CHAPTER VII

BLACKIE'S PHILOSOPHY

I did not write Norah about Von Gerhard. After all, I told myself, there was nothing to write. And so I was the first to break the solemn pact that we had made.

"You will write everything, won't you, Dawn dear?" Norah had pleaded, with tears in her pretty eyes. "Promise me. We've been nearer to each other in these last few months than we have been since we were girls. And I've loved it so. Please don't do as you did during those miserable years in New York, when you were fighting your troubles alone and we knew nothing of it. You wrote only the happy things. Promise me you'll write the unhappy ones too—though the saints forbid that there should be any to write! And Dawn, don't you dare to forget your heavy underwear in November. Those lake breezes!—Well, some one has to tell you, and I can't leave those to Von Gerhard. He has promised to act as monitor over your health."

And so I promised. I crammed my letters with descriptions of the Knapf household. I assured her that I was putting on so much weight that the skirts which formerly hung about me in limp, dejected folds now refused to meet in the back, and all the hooks and eyes were making faces at each other. My cheeks, I told her, looked as if I were wearing plumpers, and I was beginning to waddle and puff as I walked.

Norah made frantic answer:

"For mercy's sake child, be careful or you'll be FAT!"

To which I replied: "Don't care if I am. Rather be hunky and healthy than skinny and sick. Have tried both."

It is impossible to avoid becoming round-cheeked when one is working on a paper that allows one to shut one's desk and amble comfortably home for dinner at least five days in the week. Everybody is at least plump in this comfortable, gemutlich town, where everybody placidly locks his shop or office and goes home at noon to dine heavily on soup and meat and vegetables and pudding, washed down by the inevitable beer and followed by forty winks on the dining room sofa with the German Zeitung spread comfortably over the head as protection against the flies.

There is a fascination about the bright little city. There is about it something quaint and foreign, as though a cross-section of the old world had been dumped bodily into the lap of Wisconsin. It does not seem at all strange to hear German spoken everywhere—in the streets, in the shops, in the theaters, in the street cars. One day I chanced upon a sign hung above the doorway of a little German bakery over on the north side. There were Hornchen and Kaffeekuchen in the windows, and a brood of flaxen-haired and sticky children in the back of the shop. I stopped, open-mouthed, to stare at the worn sign tacked over the door.

"Hier wird Englisch gesprochen," it announced.

I blinked. Then I read it again. I shut my eyes, and opened them again suddenly. The fat German letters spoke their message as before—"English spoken here."

On reaching the office I told Norberg, the city editor, about my find. He was not impressed. Norberg never is impressed. He is the most soul-satisfying and theatrical city editor that I have ever met. He is fat, and unbelievably nimble, and keen-eyed, and untiring. He says, "Hell!" when things go wrong; he smokes innumerable cigarettes, inhaling the fumes and sending out the thin wraith of smoke with little explosive sounds between tongue and lips; he wears blue shirts, and no collar to speak of, and his trousers are kept in place only by a miracle and an inefficient looking leather belt.

When he refused to see the story in the little German bakery sign I began to argue.

"But man alive, this is America! I think I know a story when I see it. Suppose you were traveling in Germany, and should come across a sign over a shop, saying: 'Hier wird Deutsch gesprochen.' Wouldn't you think you were dreaming?"

Norberg waved an explanatory hand. "This isn't America. This is Milwaukee. After you've lived here a year or so you'll understand what I mean. If we should run a story of that sign, with a two-column cut, Milwaukee wouldn't even see the joke."

But it was not necessary that I live in Milwaukee a year or so in order to understand its peculiarities, for I had a personal conductor and efficient guide in the new friend that had come into my life with the first day of my work on the Post. Surely no woman ever had a stronger friend than little "Blackie" Griffith, sporting editor of the Milwaukee Post. We became friends, not step by step, but in one gigantic leap such as sometimes triumphs over the gap between acquaintance and liking.

I never shall forget my first glimpse of him. He strolled into the city room from his little domicile across the hall. A shabby, disreputable, out-at-elbows office coat was worn over his ultra-smart street clothes, and he was puffing at a freakish little pipe in the shape of a miniature automobile. He eyed me a moment from the doorway, a fantastic, elfin little figure. I thought that I had never seen so strange and so ugly a face as that of this little brown Welshman with his lank, black hair and his deep-set, uncanny black eyes. Suddenly he trotted over to me with a quick little step. In the doorway he had looked forty. Now a smile illumined the many lines of his dark countenance, and in some miraculous way he looked twenty.

"Are you the New York importation?" he, asked, his great black eyes searching my face.

"I'm what's left of it," I replied, meekly.

"I understand you've been in for repairs. Must of met up with somethin' on the road. They say the goin' is full of bumps in N' York."

"Bumps!" I laughed, "it's uphill every bit of the road, and yet you've got to go full speed to get anywhere. But I'm running easily again, thank you."

He waved away a cloud of pipe-smoke, and knowingly squinted through the haze. "We don't speed up much here. And they ain't no hill climbin' t' speak of. But say, if you ever should hit a nasty place on the route, toot your siren for me and I'll come. I'm a regular little human garage when it comes to patchin' up those aggravatin' screws that need oilin'. And, say, don't let Norberg bully you. My name's Blackie. I'm goin' t' like you. Come on over t' my sanctum once in a while and I'll show you my scrapbook and let you play with the office revolver."

And so it happened that I had not been in Milwaukee a month before Blackie and I were friends.

Norah was horrified. My letters were full of him. I told her that she might get a more complete mental picture of him if she knew that he wore the pinkest shirts, and the purplest neckties, and the blackest and whitest of black-and-white checked vests that ever aroused the envy of an office boy, and beneath them all, the gentlest of hearts. And therefore one loves him. There is a sort of spell about the illiterate little slangy, brown Welshman. He is the presiding genius of the place. The office boys adore him. The Old Man takes his advice in selecting a new motor car; the managing editor arranges his lunch hour to suit Blackie's and they go off to the Press club together, arm in arm. It is Blackie who lends a sympathetic ear to the society editor's tale of woe. He hires and fires the office boys; boldly he criticizes the news editor's makeup; he receives delegations of tan-coated, red-faced prizefighting-looking persons; he gently explains to the photographer why that last batch of cuts make their subjects look as if afflicted with the German measles; he arbitrates any row that the newspaper may have with such dignitaries as the mayor or the chief of police; he manages boxing shows; he skims about in a smart little roadster; he edits the best sporting page in the city; and at four o'clock of an afternoon he likes to send around the corner for a chunk of devil's food cake with butter filling from the Woman's Exchange. Blackie never went to school to speak of. He doesn't know was from were. But he can "see" a story quicker, and farther and clearer than any newspaper man I ever knew—excepting Peter Orme.

There is a legend about to the effect that one day the managing editor, who is Scotch and without a sense of humor, ordered that Blackie should henceforth be addressed by his surname of Griffith, as being a more dignified appellation for the use of fellow reporters, hangers-on, copy kids, office boys and others about the big building.

The day after the order was issued the managing editor summoned a freckled youth and thrust a sheaf of galley proofs into his hand.

"Take those to Mr. Griffith," he ordered without looking up.

"T' who?"

"To Mr. Griffith," said the managing editor, laboriously, and scowling a bit.

The boy took three unwilling steps toward the door. Then he turned a puzzled face toward the managing editor.

"Say, honest, I ain't never heard of dat guy. He must be a new one. W'ere'll I find him?"

"Oh, damn! Take those proofs to Blackie!" roared the managing editor. And thus ended Blackie's enforced flight into the realms of dignity.

All these things, and more, I wrote to the scandalized Norah. I informed her that he wore more diamond rings and scarf pins and watch fobs than a railroad conductor, and that his checked top-coat shrieked to Heaven.

There came back a letter in which every third word was underlined, and which ended by asking what the morals of such a man could be.

Then I tried to make Blackie more real to Norah who, in all her sheltered life, had never come in contact with a man like this.

"... As for his morals—or what you would consider his morals,

Sis—they probably are a deep crimson; but I'll swear there is no yellow streak. I never have heard anything more pathetic than his story. Blackie sold papers on a down-town corner when he was a baby six years old. Then he got a job as office boy here, and he used to sharpen pencils, and run errands, and carry copy. After office hours he took care of some horses in an alley barn near by, and after that work was done he was employed about the pressroom of one of the old German newspaper offices. Sometimes he would be too weary to crawl home after working half the night, and so he would fall asleep, a worn, tragic little figure, on a pile of old papers and sacks in a warm corner near the presses. He was the head of a household, and every penny counted. And all the time he was watching things, and learning. Nothing escaped those keen black eyes. He used to help the photographer when there was a pile of plates to develop, and presently he knew more about photography than the man himself. So they made him staff photographer. In some marvelous way he knew more ball players, and fighters and horsemen than the sporting editor. He had a nose for news that was nothing short of wonderful. He never went out of the office without coming back with a story. They used to use him in the sporting department when a rush was on. Then he became one of the sporting staff; then assistant sporting editor; then sporting editor. He knows this paper from the basement up. He could operate a linotype or act as managing editor with equal ease.

"No, I'm afraid that Blackie hasn't had much time for morals. But, Norah dear, I wish that you could hear him when he talks about his mother. He may follow doubtful paths, and associate with questionable people, and wear restless clothes, but I wouldn't exchange his friendship for that of a dozen of your ordinary so-called good men. All these years of work and suffering have made an old man of little Blackie, although he is young in years. But they haven't spoiled his heart any. He is able to distinguish between sham and truth because he has been obliged to do it ever since he was a child selling papers on the corner. But he still clings to the office that gave him his start, although he makes more money in a single week outside the office than his salary would amount to in half a year. He says that this is a job that does not interfere with his work."

Such is Blackie. Surely the oddest friend a woman ever had. He possesses a genius for friendship, and a wonderful understanding of suffering, born of those years of hardship and privation. Each learned the other's story, bit by bit, in a series of confidences exchanged during that peaceful, beatific period that follows just after the last edition has gone down. Blackie's little cubby-hole of an office is always blue with smoke, and cluttered with a thousand odds and ends—photographs, souvenirs, boxing-gloves, a litter of pipes and tobacco, a wardrobe of dust-covered discarded coats and hats, and Blackie in the midst of it all, sunk in the depths of his swivel chair, and looking like an amiable brown gnome, or a cheerful little joss-house god come to life. There is in him an uncanny wisdom which only the streets can teach. He is one of those born newspaper men who could not live out of sight of the ticker-tape, and the copy-hook and the proof-sheet.

"Y' see, girl, it's like this here," Blackie explained one day. "W're all workin' for some good reason. A few of us are workin' for the glory of it, and most of us are workin' t' eat, and lots of us are pluggin' an' savin' in the hopes that some day we'll have money enough to get back at some people we know; but there is some few workin' for the pure love of the work—and I guess I'm one of them fools. Y' see, I started in at this game when I was such a little runt that now it's a ingrowing habit, though it is comfortin' t' know you got a place where you c'n always come in out of the rain, and where you c'n have your mail sent."

"This newspaper work is a curse," I remarked. "Show me a clever newspaper man and I'll show you a failure. There is nothing in it but the glory—and little of that. We contrive and scheme and run about all day getting a story. And then we write it at fever heat, searching our souls for words that are cleancut and virile. And then we turn it in, and what is it? What have we to show for our day's work? An ephemeral thing, lacking the first breath of life; a thing that is dead before it is born. Why, any cub reporter, if he were to put into some other profession the same amount of nerve, and tact, and ingenuity and finesse, and stick-to-it-iveness that he expends in prying a single story out of some unwilling victim, could retire with a fortune in no time."

Blackie blew down the stem of his pipe, preparatory to refilling the bowl. There was a quizzical light in his black eyes. The little heap of burned matches at his elbow was growing to kindling wood proportions. It was common knowledge that Blackie's trick of lighting pipe or cigarette and then forgetting to puff at it caused his bill for matches to exceed his tobacco expense account.

"You talk," chuckled Blackie, "like you meant it. But sa-a-ay, girl, it's a lonesome game, this retirin' with a fortune. I've noticed that them guys who retire with a barrel of money usually dies at the end of the first year, of a kind of a lingerin' homesickness. You c'n see their pictures in th' papers, with a pathetic story of how they was just beginnin' t' enjoy life when along comes the grim reaper an' claims 'em."

Blackie slid down in his chair and blew a column of smoke ceilingward.

"I knew a guy once—newspaper man, too—who retired with a fortune. He used to do the city hall for us. Well, he got in soft with the new administration before election, and made quite a pile in stocks that was tipped off to him by his political friends. His wife was crazy for him to quit the newspaper game. He done it. An' say, that guy kept on gettin' richer and richer till even his wife was almost satisfied. But sa-a-ay, girl, was that chap lonesome! One day he come up here looking like a dog that's run off with the steak. He was just dyin' for a kind word, an' he sniffed the smell of the ink and the hot metal like it was June roses. He kind of wanders over to his old desk and slumps down in the chair, and tips it back, and puts his feet on the desk, with his hat tipped back, and a bum stogie in his mouth. And along came a kid with a bunch of papers wet from the presses and sticks one in his hand, and—well, girl, that fellow, he just wriggled he was so happy. You know as well as I do that every man on a morning paper spends his day off hanging around the office wishin' that a mob or a fire or somethin' big would tear lose so he could get back into the game. I guess I told you about the time Von Gerhard sent me abroad, didn't I?"

"Von Gerhard!" I repeated, startled. "Do you know him?"

"Well, he ain't braggin' about it none," Blackie admitted. "Von Gerhard, he told me I had about five years or so t' live, about two, three years ago. He don't approve of me. Pried into my private life, old Von Gerhard did, somethin' scand'lous. I had sort of went to pieces about that time, and I went t' him to be patched up. He thumps me fore 'an' aft, firing a volley of questions, lookin' up the roof of m' mouth, and squintin' at m' finger nails an' teeth like I was a prize horse for sale. Then he sits still, lookin' at me for about half a minute, till I begin t' feel uncomfortable. Then he says, slow: 'Young man, how old are you?'

"'O, twenty-eight or so,' I says, airy.

"'My Gawd!' said he. 'You've crammed twice those years into your life, and you'll have to pay for it. Now you listen t' me. You got t' quit workin', an' smokin', and get away from this. Take a ocean voyage,' he says, 'an' try to get four hours sleep a night, anyway.'

"Well say, mother she was scared green. So I tucked her under m' arm, and we hit it up across the ocean. Went t' Germany, knowin' that it would feel homelike there, an' we took in all the swell baden, and chased up the Jungfrau—sa-a-ay, that's a classy little mountain, that Jungfrau. Mother, she had some swell time I guess. She never set down except for meals, and she wrote picture postals like mad. But sa-a-ay, girl, was I lonesome! Maybe that trip done me good. Anyway, I'm livin' yet. I stuck it out for four months, an' that ain't so rotten for a guy who just grew up on printer's ink ever since he was old enough to hold a bunch of papers under his arm. Well, one day mother an' me was sittin' out on one of them veranda cafes they run to over there, w'en somebody hits me a crack on the shoulder, an' there stands old Ryan who used t' do A. P. here. He was foreign correspondent for some big New York syndicate papers over there.

"'Well if it ain't Blackie!' he says. 'What in Sam Hill are you doing out of your own cell when Milwaukee's just got four more games t' win the pennant?'

"Sa-a-a-ay, girl, w'en I got through huggin' him around the neck an' buyin' him drinks I knew it was me for the big ship. 'Mother,' I says, 'if you got anybody on your mind that you neglected t' send picture postals to, now's' your last chance. 'F I got to die I'm going out with m' scissors in one mitt, and m' trusty paste-pot by m' side!' An' we hits it up for old Milwaukee. I ain't been away since, except w'en I was out with the ball team, sending in sportin' extry dope for the pink sheet. The last time I was in at Baumbach's in comes Von Gerhard an'—"

"Who are Baumbach's?" I interrupted.

Blackie regarded me pityingly. "You ain't never been to Baumbach's? Why girl, if you don't know Baumbach's, you ain't never been properly introduced to Milwaukee. No wonder you ain't hep to the ways of this little community. There ain't what the s'ciety editor would call the proper ontong cordyal between you and the natives if you haven't had coffee at Baumbach's. It ain't hardly legal t' live in Milwaukee all this time without ever having been inside of B—"

"Stop! If you do not tell me at once just where this wonderful place may be found, and what one does when one finds it, and how I happened to miss it, and why it is so necessary to the proper understanding of the city—"

"I'll tell you what I'll do," said Blackie, grinning, "I'll romp you over there to-morrow afternoon at four o'clock. Ach Himmel! What will that for a grand time be, no?"

"Blackie, you're a dear to be so polite to an old married cratur' like me. Did you notice—that is, does Ernst von Gerhard drop in often at Baumbach's?"

CHAPTER VIII

KAFFEE AND KAFFEEKUCHEN

I have visited Baumbach's. I have heard Milwaukee drinking its afternoon Kaffee. O Baumbach's, with your deliciously crumbling butter cookies and your kaffee kuchen, and your thick cream, and your thicker waitresses and your cockroaches, and your dinginess and your dowdy German ladies and your black, black Kaffee, where in this country is there another like you!

Blackie, true to his promise, had hailed me from the doorway on the afternoon of the following day. In the rush of the day's work I had quite forgotten about Blackie and Baumbach's.

"Come, Kindchen!" he called. "Get your bonnet on. We will by Baumbach's go, no?"

Ruefully I gazed at the grimy cuffs of my blouse, and felt of my dishevelled hair. "Oh, I'm afraid I can't go. I look so mussy. Haven't had time to brush up."

"Brush up!" scoffed Blackie, "the only thing about you that will need brushin' up is your German. I was goin' t' warn you to rumple up your hair a little so you wouldn't feel overdressed w'en you got there. Come on, girl."

And so I came. And oh, I'm so glad I came!

I must have passed it a dozen times without once noticing it—just a dingy little black shop nestling between two taller buildings, almost within the shadow of the city hall. Over the sidewalk swung a shabby black sign with gilt letters that spelled, "Franz Baumbach."

Blackie waved an introductory hand in the direction of the

sign. "There he is. That's all you'll ever see of him."

"Dead?" asked I, regretfully, as we entered the narrow doorway.

"No; down in the basement baking Kaffeekuchen."

Two tiny show-windows faced the street—such queer, old-fashioned windows in these days of plate glass. At the back they were quite open to the shop, and in one of them reposed a huge, white, immovable structure—a majestic, heavy, nutty, surely indigestible birthday cake. Around its edge were flutings and scrolls of white icing, and on its broad breast reposed cherries, and stout butterflies of jelly, and cunning traceries of colored sugar. It was quite the dressiest cake I had ever beheld. Surely no human hand could be wanton enough to guide a knife through all that magnificence. But in the center of all this splendor was an inscription in heavy white letters of icing: "Charlottens Geburtstag."

Reluctantly I tore my gaze from this imposing example of the German confectioner's art, for Blackie was tugging impatiently at my sleeve.

"But Blackie," I marveled, "do you honestly suppose that that structure is intended for some Charlotte's birthday?"

"In Milwaukee," explained Blackie, "w'en you got a birthday you got t' have a geburtstag cake, with your name on it, and all the cousins and aunts and members of the North Side Frauen Turner Verein Gesellchaft, in for the day. It ain't considered decent if you don't. Are you ready to fight your way into the main tent?"

It was holiday time, and the single narrow aisle of the front shop was crowded. It was not easy to elbow one's way through the packed little space. Men and women were ordering recklessly of the cakes of every description that were heaped in cases and on shelves.

Cakes! What a pale; dry name to apply to those crumbling, melting, indigestible German confections! Blackie grinned with enjoyment while I gazed. There were cakes the like of which I had never seen and of which I did not even know the names. There were little round cup cakes made of almond paste that melts in the mouth; there were Schnecken glazed with a delicious candied brown sugar; there were Bismarcks composed of layer upon layer of flaky crust inlaid with an oozy custard that evades the eager consumer at the first bite, and that slides down one's collar when chased with a pursuing tongue. There were Pfeffernusse; there, were Lebkuchen; there were cheese-kuchen; plum-kuchen, peach-kuchen, Apfelkuchen, the juicy fruit stuck thickly into the crust, the whole dusted over with powdered sugar. There were Torten, and Hornchen, and butter cookies.

Blackie touched my arm, and I tore my gaze from a cherry-studded Schaumtorte that was being reverently packed for delivery.

"My, what a greedy girl! Now get your mind all made up. This is your chance. You know you're supposed t' take a slant at th' things an' make up your mind w'at you want before you go back w'ere th' tables are. Don't fumble this thing. When Olga or Minna comes waddlin' up t' you an' says: 'Nu, Fraulein?' you gotta tell her whether your heart says plum-kuchen oder Nusstorte, or both, see? Just like that. Now make up your mind. I'd hate t' have you blunder. Have you decided?"

"Decided! How can I?" I moaned, watching a black-haired, black-eyed Alsatian girl behind the counter as she rolled a piece of white paper into a cone and dipped a spoonful of whipped cream from a great brown bowl heaped high with the snowy stuff. She filled the paper cone, inserted the point of it into one end of a hollow pastry horn, and gently squeezed. Presto! A cream-filled Hornchen!

"Oh, Blackie!" I gasped. "Come on. I want to go in and eat."

As we elbowed our way to the rear room separated from the front shop only by a flimsy wooden partition, I expected I know not what.

But surely this was not Blackie's much-vaunted Baumbach's!

This long, narrow, dingy room, with its bare floor and its iron-legged tables whose bare marble tops were yellow with age and use! I said nothing as we seated ourselves. Blackie was watching me out of the tail of his eye. My glance wandered about the shabby, smoke-filled room, and slowly and surely the charm of that fusty, dingy little cafe came upon me.

A huge stove glowed red in one corner. On the wall behind the stove was suspended a wooden rack, black with age, its compartments holding German, Austrian and Hungarian newspapers. Against the opposite wall stood an ancient walnut mirror, and above it hung a colored print of Bismarck, helmeted, uniformed, and fiercely mustached. The clumsy iron-legged tables stood in two solemn rows down the length of the narrow room. Three or four stout, blond girls plodded back and forth, from tables to front shop, bearing trays of cakes and steaming cups of coffee. There was a rumble and clatter of German. Every one seemed to know every one else. A game of chess was in progress at one table, and between moves each contestant would refresh himself with a long-drawn, sibilant mouthful of coffee. There was nothing about the place or its occupants to remind one of America. This dim, smoky, cake-scented cafe was Germany.

"Time!" said Blackie. "Here comes Rosie to take our order. You can take your choice of coffee or chocolate. That's as fancy as they get here."

An expansive blond girl paused at our table smiling a broad welcome at Blackie.

"Wie geht's, Roschen?" he greeted her. Roschen's smile became still more pervasive, so that her blue eyes disappeared in creases of good humor. She wiped the marble table top with a large and careless gesture that precipitated stray crumbs into our laps. "Gut!" murmured she, coyly, and leaned one hand on a portly hip in an attitude of waiting.

"Coffee?" asked Blackie, turning to me. I nodded.

"Zweimal Kaffee?" beamed Roschen, grasping the idea.

"Now's your time to speak up," urged Blackie. "Go ahead an' order all the cream gefillte things that looked good to you out in front."

But I leaned forward, lowering my voice discreetly. "Blackie, before I plunge in too recklessly, tell me, are their prices very—"

"Sa-a-ay, child, you just can't spend half a dollar here if you try. The flossiest kind of thing they got is only ten cents a order. They'll smother you in whipped cream f'r a quarter. You c'n come in here an' eat an' eat an' put away piles of cakes till you feel like a combination of Little Jack Horner an' old Doc Johnson. An' w'en you're all through, they hand yuh your check, an', say—it says forty-five cents. You can't beat it, so wade right in an' spoil your complexion."

With enthusiasm I turned upon the patient Rosie. "O, bring me some of those cunning little round things with the cream on 'em, you know—two of those, eh Blackie? And a couple of those with the flaky crust and the custard between, and a slice of that fluffy-looking cake and some of those funny cocked-hat shaped cookies—"

But a pall of bewilderment was slowly settling over Rosie's erstwhile smiling face. Her plump shoulders went up in a helpless shrug, and she turned her round blue eyes appealingly to Blackie.

"Was meint sie alles?" she asked.

So I began all over again, with the assistance of Blackie. We went into minute detail. We made elaborate gestures. We drew pictures of our desired goodies on the marble-topped table, using a soft-lead pencil. Rosie's countenance wore a distracted look. In desperation I was about to accompany her to the crowded shop, there to point out my chosen dainties when suddenly, as they would put it here, a light went her over.

"Ach, yes-s-s-s! Sie wollten vielleicht abgeruhrter Gugelhopf haben, und auch Schaumtorte, und Bismarcks, und Hornchen mit cream gefullt, nicht?"

"Certainly," I murmured, quite crushed. Roschen waddled merrily off to the shop.

Blackie was rolling a cigarette. He ran his funny little red tongue along the edge of the paper and glanced up at me in glee. "Don't bother about me," he generously observed. "Just set still and let the atmosphere soak in."

But already I was lost in contemplation of a red-faced, pompadoured German who was drinking coffee and reading the Fliegende Blatter at a table just across the way. There were counterparts of my aborigines at Knapf's—thick spectacled engineers with high foreheads—actors and actresses from the German stock company—reporters from the English and German newspapers—business men with comfortable German consciences—long-haired musicians—dapper young lawyers—a giggling group of college girls and boys—a couple of smartly dressed women nibbling appreciatively at slices of Nusstorte—low-voiced lovers whose coffee cups stood untouched at their elbows, while no fragrant cloud of steam rose to indicate that there was warmth within. Their glances grow warmer as the neglected Kaffee grows colder. The color comes and goes in the girl's face and I watch it, a bit enviously, marveling that the old story still should be so new.

At a large square table near the doorway a group of eight men were absorbed in an animated political discussion, accompanied by much waving of arms, and thundering of gutturals. It appeared to be a table of importance, for the high-backed bench that ran along one side was upholstered in worn red velvet, and every newcomer paused a moment to nod or to say a word in greeting. It was not of American politics that they talked, but of the politics of Austria and Hungary. Finally the argument resolved itself into a duel of words between a handsome, red-faced German whose rosy skin seemed to take on a deeper tone in contrast to the whiteness of his hair and mustache, and a swarthy young fellow whose thick spectacles and heavy mane of black hair gave him the look of a caricature out of an illustrated German weekly. The red-faced man argued loudly, with much rapping of bare knuckles on the table top. But the dark man spoke seldom, and softly, with a little twisted half-smile on his lips; and whenever he spoke the red-faced man grew redder, and there came a huge laugh from the others who sat listening.

"Say, wouldn't it curdle your English?" Blackie laughed.

Solemnly I turned to him. "Blackie Griffith, these people do not even realize that there is anything unusual about this."

"Sure not; that's the beauty of it. They don't need to make no artificial atmosphere for this place; it just grows wild, like dandelions. Everybody comes here for their coffee because their aunts an' uncles and Grossmutters and Grosspapas used t' come, and come yet, if they're livin'! An', after all, what is it but a little German bakery?"

"But O, wise Herr Baumbach down in the kitchen! O, subtle Frau Baumbach back of the desk!" said I. "Others may fit their shops with mirrors, and cut-glass chandeliers and Oriental rugs and mahogany, but you sit serenely by, and you smile, and you change nothing. You let the brown walls grow dimmer with age; you see the marble-topped tables turning yellow; you leave bare your wooden floor, and you smile, and smile, and smile."

"Fine!" applauded Blackie. "You're on. And here comes Rosie."

Rosie, the radiant, placed on the table cups and saucers of an unbelievable thickness. She set them down on the marble surface with a crash as one who knows well that no mere marble or granite could shatter the solidity of those stout earthenware receptacles. Napkins there were none. I was to learn that fingers were rid of any clinging remnants of cream or crumb by the simple expedient of licking them.

Blackie emptied his pitcher of cream into his cup of black, black coffee, sugared it, stirred, tasted, and then, with a wicked gleam in his black eyes he lifted the heavy cup to his lips and took a long, gurgling mouthful.

"Blackie," I hissed, "if you do that again I shall refuse to speak to you!"

"Do what?" demanded he, all injured innocence.

"Snuffle up your coffee like that."

"Why, girl, that's th' proper way t' drink coffee here. Listen t' everybody else." And while I glared he wrapped his hand lovingly about his cup, holding the spoon imprisoned between first and second fingers, and took another sibilant mouthful. "Any more of your back talk and I'll drink it out of m' saucer an' blow on it like the hefty party over there in the earrings is doin'. Calm yerself an' try a Bismarck."

I picked up one of the flaky confections and eyed it in despair. There were no plates except that on which the cakes reposed.

"How does one eat them?" I inquired.

"Yuh don't really eat 'em. The motion is more like inhalin'. T' eat 'em successful you really ought t' get into a bath-tub half-filled with water, because as soon's you bite in at one end w'y the custard stuff slides out at the other, an' no human mouth c'n be two places at oncet. Shut your eyes girl, an' just wade in."

I waded. In silence I took a deep delicious bite, nimbly chased the coy filling around a corner with my tongue, devoured every bit down to the last crumb and licked the stickiness off my fingers. Then I investigated the interior of the next cake.

"I'm coming here every day," I announced.

"Better not. Ruin your complexion and turn all your lines into bumps. Look at the dame with the earrings. I've been keepin' count an' I've seen her eat three Schnecken, two cream puffs, a Nusshornchen and a slice of Torte with two cups of coffee. Ain't she a horrible example! And yet she's got th' nerve t' wear a princess gown!"

"I don't care," I replied, recklessly, my voice choked with whipped cream and butteriness. "I can just feel myself getting greasy. Haven't I done beautifully for a new hand? Now tell me about some of these people. Who is the funny little man in the checked suit with the black braid trimming, and the green cravat, and the white spats, and the tan hat and the eyeglasses?"

"Ain't them th' dizzy habiliments?" A note of envy crept into Blackie's voice. "His name is Hugo Luders. Used t' be a reporter on the Germania, but he's reformed and gone into advertisin', where there's real money. Some say he wears them clo'es on a bet, and some say his taste in dress is a curse descended upon him from Joseph, the guy with the fancy coat, but I think he wears 'em because he fancies 'em. He's been coming here ever' afternoon for twelve years, has a cup of coffee, game of chess, and a pow-wow with a bunch of cronies. If Baumbach's ever decide to paint the front of their shop or put in cut glass fixtures and handpainted china, Hugo Luders would serve an injunction on 'em. Next!"

"Who's the woman with the leathery complexion and the belt to match, and the untidy hair and the big feet? I like her face. And why does she sit at a table with all those strange-looking men? And who are all the men? And who is the fur-lined grand opera tenor just coming in—Oh!"

Blackie glanced over his shoulder just as the tall man in the doorway turned his face toward us. "That? Why, girl, that's Von Gerhard, the man who gives me one more year t' live. Look at everybody kowtowing to him. He don't favor Baumbach's often. Too busy patching up the nervous wrecks that are washed up on his shores."

The tall figure in the doorway was glancing from table to table, nodding here and there to an acquaintance. His eyes traveled the length of the room. Now they were nearing us. I felt a sudden, inexplicable tightening at heart and throat, as though fingers were clutching there. Then his eyes met mine, and I felt the blood rushing to my face as he came swiftly over to our table and took my hand in his.

"So you have discovered Baumbach's," he said. "May I have my coffee and cigar here with you?"

"Blackie here is responsible for my being initiated into the sticky mysteries of Baumbach's. I never should have discovered it if he had not offered to act as personal conductor. You know one another, I believe?"

The two men shook hands across the table. There was something forced and graceless about the act. Blackie eyed

Von Gerhard through a misty curtain of cigarette smoke. Von Gerhard gazed at Blackie through narrowed lids as he lighted his cigar. "I'm th' gink you killed off two or three years back," Blackie explained.

"I remember you perfectly," Von Gerhard returned, courteously. "I rejoice to see that I was mistaken."

"Well," drawled Blackie, a wicked gleam in his black eyes, "I'm some rejoiced m'self, old top. Angel wings and a white kimono, worn bare-footy, would go some rotten with my Spanish style of beauty, what? Didn't know that you and m'dame friend here was acquainted. Known each other long?"

I felt myself flushing again.

"I knew Dr. von Gerhard back home. I've scarcely seen him since I have been here. Famous specialists can't be bothered with middle-aged relatives of their college friends, can they, Herr Doktor?"

And now it was Von Gerhard's face that flushed a deep and painful crimson. He looked at me, in silence, and I felt very little, and insignificant, and much like an impudent child who has stuck out its tongue at its elders. Silent men always affect talkative women in that way.

"You know that what you say is not true," he said, slowly.

"Well, we won't quibble. We—we were just about to leave, weren't we Blackie?"

"Just," said Blackie, rising. "Sorry t' see you drinkin' Baumbach's coffee, Doc. It ain't fair t' your patients."

"Quite right," replied Von Gerhard; and rose with us. "I shall not drink it. I shall walk home with Mrs. Orme instead, if she will allow me. That will be more stimulating than coffee, and twice as dangerous, perhaps, but—"

"You know how I hate that sort of thing," I said, coldly, as we passed from the warmth of the little front shop where the plump girls were still filling pasteboard boxes with holiday cakes, to the brisk chill of the winter street. The little black-and-gilt sign swung and creaked in the wind. Whimsically, and with the memory of that last cream-filled cake fresh in my mind, I saluted the letters that spelled "Franz Baumbach."

Blackie chuckled impishly. "Just the same, try a pinch of soda bicarb'nate when you get home, Dawn," he advised. "Well, I'm off to the factory again. Got t' make up for time wasted on m' lady friend. Auf wiedersehen!"

And the little figure in the checked top-coat trotted off.

"But he called you—Dawn," broke from Von Gerhard.

"Mhum," I agreed. "My name's Dawn."

"Surely not to him. You have known him but a few weeks. I would not have presumed—"

"Blackie never presumes," I laughed. "Blackie's just—Blackie. Imagine taking offense at him! He knows every one by their given name, from Jo, the boss of the pressroom, to the Chief, who imports his office coats from London. Besides, Blackie and I are newspaper men. And people don't scrape and bow in a newspaper office—especially when they're fond of one another. You wouldn't understand."

As I looked at Von Gerhard in the light of the street lamp I saw a tense, drawn look about the little group of muscles which show when the teeth are set hard. When he spoke those muscles had relaxed but little.

"One man does not talk ill of another. But this is different. I want to ask you—do you know what manner of man this—this Blackie is? I ask you because I would have you safe and sheltered always from such as he—because I—"

"Safe! From Blackie? Now listen. There never was a safer, saner, truer, more generous friend. Oh, I know what his life has been. But what else could it have been, beginning as he did? I have no wish to reform him. I tried my hand at reforming one man, and made a glorious mess of it. So I'll just take Blackie as he is, if you please—slang, wickedness, pink shirt, red necktie, diamond rings and all. If there's any bad in him, we all know it, for it's right down on the table, face up. You're just angry because he called you Doc."

"Small one," said Von Gerhard, in his quaint German idiom, "we will not quarrel, you and I. If I have been neglectful it was because edged tools were never a chosen plaything of mine. Perhaps your little Blackie realizes that he need have no fear of such things, for the Great Fear is upon him."

"The Great Fear! You mean!—"

"I mean that there are too many fine little lines radiating from the corners of the sunken eyes, and that his hand-clasp leaves a moisture in the palm. Ach! you may laugh. Come, we will change the subject to something more cheerful, yes? Tell me, how grows the book?"

"By inches. After working all day on a bulletin paper whose city editor is constantly shouting: 'Boil it now, fellows! Keep it down! We're crowded!' it is too much of a wrench to find myself seated calmly before my own typewriter at night, privileged to write one hundred thousand words if I choose. I can't get over the habit of crowding the story all into the first paragraph. Whenever I flower into a descriptive passage I glance nervously over my shoulder, expecting to find Norberg stationed behind me, scissors and blue pencil in hand. Consequently the book, thus far, sounds very much like a police reporter's story of a fire four minutes before the paper is due to go to press."

Von Gerhard's face was unsmiling. "So," he said, slowly. "You burn the candle at both ends. All day you write, is it not so? And at night you come home to write still more? Ach, Kindchen!— Na, we shall change all that. We will be better comrades, we two, yes? You remember that gay little walk of last autumn, when we explored the Michigan country lane at dusk? I shall be your Sunday Schatz, and there shall be more rambles like that one, to bring the roses into your cheeks. We shall be good Kameraden, as you and this little Griffith are—what is it they say—good fellows? That is it—good fellows, yes? So, shall we shake hands on it?"

But I snatched my hand away. "I don't want to be a good fellow," I cried. "I'm tired of being a good fellow. I've been a good fellow for years and years, while every other married woman in the world has been happy in her own home, bringing up her babies. When I am old I want some sons to worry me, too, and to stay awake nights for, and some daughters to keep me young, and to prevent me from doing my hair in a knob and wearing bonnets! I hate good-fellow women, and so do you, and so does every one else! I—I—"

"Dawn!" cried Von Gerhard. But I ran up the steps and into the house and slammed the door behind me, leaving him standing there.

CHAPTER IX

THE LADY FROM VIENNA

Two more aborigines have appeared. One of them is a lady aborigine. They made their entrance at supper and I forgot to eat, watching them. The new-comers are from Vienna. He is an expert engineer and she is a woman of noble birth, with a history. Their combined appearance is calculated to strike terror to the heart. He is daringly ugly, with a chin that curves in under his lip and then out in a peak, like pictures of Punch. She wore a gray gown of a style I never had seen before and never expect to see again. It was fastened with huge black buttons all the way down the breathlessly tight front, and the upper part was composed of that pre-historic garment known as a basque. She curved in where she should have curved out, and she bulged where she should have had "lines." About her neck was suspended a string of cannon-ball beads that clanked as she walked. On her forehead rested a sparse fringe.

"Mein Himmel!" thought I. "Am I dreaming? This isn't Wisconsin. This is Nurnberg, or Strassburg, with a dash of Heidelberg and Berlin thrown in. Dawn, old girl, it's going to be more instructive than a Cook's tour."

That turned out to be the truest prophecy I ever made.

The first surprising thing that the new-comers did was to seat themselves at the long table with the other aborigines, the lady aborigine being the only woman among the twelve men. It was plain that they had known one another previous to this meeting, for they became very good friends at once, and the men grew heavily humorous about there being thirteen at table.

At that the lady aborigine began to laugh. Straightway I forgot the outlandish gown, forgot the cannon-ball beads, forgot the sparse fringe, forgave the absence of "lines." Such a voice! A lilting, melodious thing. She broke into a torrent of speech, with bewildering gestures, and I saw that her hands were exquisitely formed and as expressive as her voice. Her German was the musical tongue of the Viennese, possessing none of the gutturals and sputterings. When she crowned it with the gay little trilling laugh my views on the language underwent a lightning change. It seemed the most natural thing in the world to see her open the flat, silver case that dangled at the end of the cannon-ball chain, take out a cigarette, light it, and smoke it there in that little German dining room. She wore the most gracefully nonchalant air imaginable as she blew little rings and wreaths, and laughed and chatted brightly with her husband and the other men. Occasionally she broke into French, her accent as charmingly perfect as it had been in her native tongue. There was a moment of breathless staring on the part of the respectable middle-class Frauen at the other tables. Then they shrugged their shoulders and plunged into their meal again. There was a certain little high-born air of assurance about that cigarette-smoking that no amount of staring could ruffle.

Watching the new aborigines grew to be a sort of game. The lady aborigine of the golden voice, and the ugly husband of the peaked chin had a strange fascination for me. I scrambled downstairs at meal time in order not to miss them, and I dawdled over the meal so that I need not leave before they. I discovered that when the lady aborigine was animated, her face was that of a young woman, possessing a certain high-bred charm, but that when in repose the face of the lady aborigine was that of a very old and tired woman indeed. Also that her husband bullied her, and that when he did that she looked at him worshipingly.

Then one evening, a week or so after the appearance of the new aborigines, there came a clumping at my door. I was seated at my typewriter and the book was balkier than usual, and I wished that the clumper at the door would go away.

"Come!" I called, ungraciously enough. Then, on second thought: "Herein!"

The knob turned slowly, and the door opened just enough to admit the top of a head crowned with a tight, moist German knob of hair. I searched my memory to recognize the knob, failed utterly and said again, this time with mingled curiosity and hospitality:

"Won't you come in?"

The apparently bodiless head thrust itself forward a bit, disclosing an apologetically smiling face, with high check bones that glistened with friendliness and scrubbing.

"Nabben', Fraulein," said the head.

"Nabben'," I replied, more mystified than ever. "Howdy do! Is there anything—"

The head thrust itself forward still more, showing a pair of plump shoulders as its support. Then the plump shoulders heaved into the room, disclosing a stout, starched gingham body.

"Ich bin Frau Knapf," announced the beaming vision.

Now up to this time Frau Knapf had maintained a Mrs. Harris-like mysteriousness. I had heard rumors of her, and I had partaken of certain crispy dishes of German extraction, reported to have come from her deft hands, but I had not even caught a glimpse of her skirts whisking around a corner.

Therefore: "Frau Knapf!" I repeated. "Nonsense! There ain't no sich person—that is, I'm glad to see you. Won't you come in and sit down?"

"Ach, no!" smiled the substantial Frau Knapf, clinging tightly to the door knob. "I got no time. It gives much to do to-night yet. Kuchen dough I must set, und ich weiss nicht was. I got no time."

Bustling, red-cheeked Frau Knapf! This was why I had never had a glimpse of her. Always, she got no time. For while Herr Knapf, dapper and genial, welcomed new-comers, chatted with the diners, poured a glass of foaming Doppel-brau for Herr Weber or, dexterously carved fowl for the aborigines' table, Frau Knapf was making the wheels go round. I discovered that it was she who bakes the melting, golden German Pfannkuchen on Sunday mornings; she it is who fries the crisp and hissing Wienerschnitzel; she it is who prepares the plump ducklings, and the thick gravies, and the steaming lentil soup and the rosy sausages nestling coyly in their bed of sauerkraut. All the week Frau Knapf bakes and broils and stews, her rosy cheeks taking on a twinkling crimson from the fire over which she bends. But on Sunday night Frau Knapf sheds her huge apron and rolls down the sleeves from her plump arms. On Sunday evening she leaves pots and pans and cooking, and is a transformed Frau Knapf. Then does she don a bright blue silk waist and a velvet coat that is dripping with jet, and a black bonnet on which are perched palpitating birds and weary-looking plumes. Then she and Herr Knapf walk comfortably down to the Pabst theater to see the German play by the German stock company. They applaud their favorite stout, blond, German comedienne as she romps through the acts of a sprightly German comedy, and after the play they go to their favorite Wein-stube around the corner. There they have sardellen and cheese sandwiches and a great deal of beer, and for one charmed evening Frau Knapf forgets all about the insides of geese and the thickening for gravies, and is happy.

Many of these things Frau Knapf herself told me, standing there by the door with the Kuchen heavy on her mind. Some of them I got from Ernst von Gerhard when I told him about my visitor and her errand. The errand was not disclosed until Frau Knapf had caught me casting a despairing glance at my last typewritten page.

"Ach, see! you got no time for talking to, ain't it?" she apologized.

"Heaps of time," I politely assured her, "don't hurry. But why not have a chair and be comfortable?"

Frau Knapf was not to be deceived. "I go in a minute. But first it is something I like to ask you. You know maybe Frau Nirlanger?"

I shook my head.

"But sure you must know. From Vienna she is, with such a voice like a bird."

"And the beads, and the gray gown, and the fringe, and the cigarettes?"

"And the oogly husband," finished Frau Knapf, nodding.

"Oogly," I agreed, "isn't the name for it. And so she is Frau Nirlanger? I thought there would be a Von at the very least."

Whereupon my visitor deserted the doorknob, took half a dozen stealthy steps in my direction and lowered her voice to a hissing whisper of confidence.

"It is more as a Von. I will tell you. Today comes Frau Nirlanger by me and she says: 'Frau Knapf, I wish to buy clothes, aber echt Amerikanische. Myself, I do not know what is modish, and I cannot go alone to buy.'"

"That's a grand idea," said I, recalling the gray basque and the cannon-ball beads.

"Ja, sure it is," agreed Frau Knapf. "Soo-o-o, she asks me was it some lady who would come with her by the stores to help a hat and suit and dresses to buy. Stylish she likes they should be, and echt Amerikanisch. So-o-o-o, I say to her, I would go myself with you, only so awful stylish I ain't, and anyway I got no time. But a lady I know who is got such stylish clothes!" Frau Knapf raised admiring hands and eyes toward heaven. "Such a nice lady she is, and stylish, like anything! And her name is Frau Orme."

"Oh, really, Frau Knapf—" I murmured in blushing confusion.

"Sure, it is so," insisted Frau Knapf, coming a step nearer, and sinking her, voice one hiss lower. "You shouldn't say I said it, but Frau Nirlanger likes she should look young for her husband. He is much younger as she is—aber much. Anyhow ten years. Frau Nirlanger does not tell me this, but from other people I have found out." Frau Knapf shook her head mysteriously a great many times. "But maybe you ain't got such an interest in Frau Nirlanger, yes?"

"Interest! I'm eaten up with curiosity. You shan't leave this room alive until you've told me!"

Frau Knapf shook with silent mirth. "Now you make jokings, ain't? Well, I tell you. In Vienna, Frau Nirlanger was a widow, from a family aber hoch edel—very high born. From the court her family is, and friends from the Emperor, und alles. Sure! Frau Nirlanger, she is different from the rest. Books she likes, und meetings, und all such komisch things. And what you think!"

"I don't know," I gasped, hanging on her words, "what DO I think?"

"She meets this here Konrad Nirlanger, and falls with him in love. Und her family is mad! But schrecklich mad! Forty years old she is, and from a noble family, and Konrad Nirlanger is only a student from a university, and he comes from the Volk. Sehr gebildet he is, but not high born. So-o-o-o-o, she runs with him away and is married."

Shamelessly I drank it all in. "You don't mean it! Well, then what happened? She ran away with him—with that chin! and then what?"

Frau Knapf was enjoying it as much as I. She drew a long breath, felt of the knob of hair, and plunged once more into the story.

"Like a story-book it is, nicht? Well, Frau Nirlanger, she has already a boy who is ten years old, and a fine sum of money that her first husband left her. Aber when she runs with this poor kerl away from her family, and her first husband's family is so schrecklich mad that they try by law to take from her her boy and her money, because she has her highborn family disgraced, you see? For a year they fight in the courts, and then it stands that her money Frau Nirlanger can keep, but her boy she cannot have. He will be taken by her highborn family and educated, and he must forget all about his mamma. To cry it is, ain't it? Das arme Kind! Well, she can stand it no longer to live where her boy is, and not to see him. So-o-o-o, Konrad Nirlanger he gets a chance to come by Amerika where there is a big engineering plant here in Milwaukee, and she begs her husband he should come, because this boy she loves very much—Oh, she loves her young husband too, but different, yes?"

"Oh, yes," I agreed, remembering the gay little trilling laugh, and the face that was so young when animated, and so old and worn in repose. "Oh, yes. Quite, quite different."

Frau Knapf smoothed her spotless skirt and shook her head slowly and sadly. "So-o-o-o, by Amerika they come. And Konrad Nirlanger he is maybe a little cross and so, because for a year they have been in the courts, and it might have been the money they would lose, and for money Konrad Nirlanger cares—well, you shall see. But Frau Nirlanger must not mourn and cry. She must laugh and sing, and be gay for her husband. But Frau Nirlanger has no grand clothes, for first she runs away with Konrad Nirlanger, and then her money is tied in the law. Now she has again her money, and she must be young—but young!"

With a gesture that expressed a world of pathos and futility Frau Knapf flung out her arms. "He must not see that she looks different as the ladies in this country. So Frau Nirlanger wants she should buy here in the stores new dresses—echt Amerikanische. All new and beautiful things she would have, because she must look young, ain't it? And perhaps her boy will remember her when he is a fine young man, if she is yet young when he grows up, you see? And too, there is the young husband. First, she gives up her old life, and her friends and her family for this man, and then she must do all things to keep him. Men, they are but children, after all," spake the wise Frau Knapf in conclusion. "They war and cry and plead for that which they would have, and when they have won, then see! They are amused for a moment, and the new toy is thrown aside."

"Poor, plain, vivacious, fascinating little Frau Nirlanger!" I said. "I wonder just how much of pain and heartache that little musical laugh of hers conceals?"

"Ja, that is so," mused Frau Knapf. "Her eyes look like eyes that have wept much, not? And so you will be so kind and go maybe to select the so beautiful clothes?"

"Clothes?" I repeated, remembering the original errand. "But dear lady! How, does one select clothes for a woman of forty who would not weary her husband? That is a task for a French modiste, a wizard, and a fairy godmother all rolled into one."

"But you will do it, yes?" urged Frau Knapf.

"I'll do it," I agreed, a bit ruefully, "if only to see the face of the oogly husband when his bride is properly corseted and shod."

Whereupon Frau Knapf, in a panic, remembered the unset Kuchen dough and rushed away, with her hand on her lips and her eyes big with secrecy. And I sat staring at the last typewritten page stuck in my typewriter and I found that the little letters on the white page were swimming in a dim purple haze.

CHAPTER X

A TRAGEDY OF GOWNS

From husbands in general, and from oogly German husbands in particular may Hymen defend me! Never again will I attempt to select "echt Amerikanische" clothes for a woman who must not weary her young husband. But how was I to know that the harmless little shopping expedition would resolve itself into a domestic tragedy, with Herr Nirlanger as the villain, Frau Nirlanger as the persecuted heroine, and I as—what is it in tragedy that corresponds to the innocent bystander in real life? That would be my role.

The purchasing of the clothes was a real joy. Next to buying pretty things for myself there is nothing I like better than choosing them for some one else. And when that some one else happens to be a fascinating little foreigner who coos over the silken stuffs in a delightful mixture of German and English; and especially when that some one else must be made to look so charming that she will astonish her oogly husband, then does the selecting of those pretty things cease to be a task, and become an art.

It was to be a complete surprise to Herr Nirlanger. He was to know nothing of it until everything was finished and Frau Nirlanger, dressed in the prettiest of the pretty Amerikanisch gowns, was ready to astound him when he should come home from the office of the vast plant where he solved engineering problems.

"From my own money I buy all this," Frau Nirlanger confided to me, with a gay little laugh of excitement, as we started out.

"From Vienna it comes. Always I have given it at once to my husband, as a wife should. Yesterday it came, but I said nothing, and when my husband said to me, 'Anna, did not the money come as usual to-day? It is time,' I told a little lie—but a little one, is it not? Very amusing it was. Almost I did laugh. Na, he will not be cross when he see how his wife like the Amerikanische ladies will look. He admires very much the ladies of Amerika. Many times he has said so."

("I'll wager he has—the great, ugly boor!" I thought, in parenthesis.) "We'll show him!" I said, aloud. "He won't know you. Such a lot of beautiful clothes as we can buy with all this money. Oh, dear Frau Nirlanger, it's going to be slathers of fun! I feel as excited about it as though it were a trousseau we were buying."

"So it is," she replied, a little shadow of sadness falling across the brightness of her face. "I had no proper clothes when we were married—but nothing! You know perhaps my story. In America, everyone knows everything. It is wonderful. When I ran away to marry Konrad Nirlanger I had only the dress which I wore; even that I borrowed from one of the upper servants, on a pretext, so that no one should recognize me. Ach Gott! I need not have worried. So! You see, it will be after all a trousseau."

Why, oh, why should a woman with her graceful carriage and pretty vivacity have been cursed with such an ill-assorted lot of features! Especially when certain boorish young husbands have expressed an admiration for pink-and-white effects in femininity.

"Never mind, Mr. Husband, I'll show yez!" I resolved as the elevator left us at the floor where waxen ladies in shining glass cases smiled amiably all the day.

There must be no violent pinks or blues. Brown was too old. She was not young enough for black. Violet was too trying. And so the gowns began to strew tables and chairs and racks, and still I shook my head, and Frau Nirlanger looked despairing, and the be-puffed and real Irish-crocheted saleswoman began to develop a baleful gleam about the eyes.

And then we found it! It was a case of love at first sight. The unimaginative would have called it gray. The thoughtless would have pronounced it pink. It was neither, and both; a soft, rosily-gray mixture of the two, like the sky that one sometimes sees at winter twilight, the pink of the sunset veiled by the gray of the snow clouds. It was of a supple, shining cloth, simple in cut, graceful in lines.

"There! We've found it. Let's pray that it will not require too much altering."

But when it had been slipped over her head we groaned at the inadequacy of her old-fashioned stays. There followed a flying visit to the department where hips were whisked out of sight in a jiffy, and where lines miraculously took the place of curves. Then came the gown once more, over the new stays this time. The effect was magical. The Irish-crocheted saleswoman and I clasped hands and fell back in attitudes of admiration. Frau Nirlanger turned this way and that before the long mirror and chattered like a pleased child. Her adjectives grew into words of six syllables. She cooed over the soft-shining stuff in little broken exclamations in French and German.

Then came a straight and simple street suit of blue cloth, a lingerie gown of white, hats, shoes and even a couple of limp satin petticoats. The day was gone before we could finish.

I bullied them into promising the pinky-gray gown for the next afternoon.

"Sooch funs!" giggled Frau Nirlanger, "and how it makes one tired. So kind you were, to take this trouble for me. Me, I could never have warred with that Fraulein who served us—so haughty she was, nicht? But it is good again pretty clothes to have. Pretty gowns I lofe—you also, not?"

"Indeed I do lofe 'em. But my money comes to me in a yellow pay envelope, and it is spent before it reaches me, as a rule. It doesn't leave much of a margin for general recklessness."

A tiny sigh came from Frau Nirlanger. "There will be little

to give to Konrad this time. So much money they cost, those clothes! But Konrad, he will not care when he sees the so beautiful dresses, is it not so?"

"Care!" I cried with a great deal of bravado, although a tiny inner voice spake in doubt. "Certainly not. How could he?"

Next day the boxes came, and we smuggled them into my room. The unwrapping of the tissue paper folds was a ceremony. We reveled in the very crackle of it. I had scuttled home from the office as early as decency would permit, in order to have plenty of time for the dressing. It must be quite finished before Herr Nirlanger should arrive. Frau Nirlanger had purchased three tickets for the German theater, also as a surprise, and I was to accompany the happily surprised husband and the proud little wife of the new Amerikanische clothes.

I coaxed her to let me do things to her hair. Usually she wore a stiff and ugly coiffure that could only be described as a chignon. I do not recollect ever having seen a chignon, but I know that it must look like that. I was thankful for my Irish deftness of fingers as I stepped back to view the result of my labors. The new arrangement of the hair gave her features a new softness and dignity.

We came to the lacing of the stays, with their exaggerated length. "Aber!" exclaimed Frau Nirlanger, not daring to laugh because of the strange snugness. "Ach!" and again, "Aber to laugh it is!"

We had decided the prettiest of the new gowns must do honor to the occasion. "This shade is called ashes of roses," I explained, as I slipped it over her head.

"Ashes of roses!" she echoed. "How pretty, yes? But a little sad too, is it not so? Like rosy hopes that have been withered. Ach, what a foolish talk! So, now you will fasten it please. A real trick it is to button such a dress—so sly they are, those fastenings."

When all the sly fastenings were secure I stood at gaze.

"Nose is shiny," I announced, searching in a drawer for chamois and powder.

Frau Nirlanger raised an objecting hand. "But Konrad does not approve of such things. He has said so. He has—"

"You tell your Konrad that a chamois skin isn't half as objectionable as a shiny one. Come here and let me dust this over your nose and chin, while I breathe a prayer of thanks that I have no overzealous husband near to forbid me the use of a bit of powder. There! If I sez it mesilf as shouldn't, yez ar-r-re a credit t' me, me darlint."

"You are satisfied. There is not one small thing awry? Ach, how we shall laugh at Konrad's face."

"Satisfied! I'd kiss you if I weren't afraid that I should muss you up. You're not the same woman. You look like a girl! And so pretty! Now skedaddle into your own rooms, but don't you dare to sit down for a moment. I'm going down to get Frau Knapf before your husband arrives."

"But is there then time?" inquired Frau Nirlanger. "He should be here now."

"I'll bring her up in a jiffy, just for one peep. She won't know you! Her face will be a treat! Don't touch your hair—it's quite perfect. And f'r Jawn's sake! Don't twist around to look at yourself in the back or something will burst, I know it will. I'll be back in a minute. Now run!"

The slender, graceful figure disappeared with a gay little laugh, and I flew downstairs for Frau Knapf. She was discovered with a spoon in one hand and a spluttering saucepan in the other. I detached her from them, clasped her big, capable red hands and dragged her up the stairs, explaining as I went.

"Now don't fuss about that supper! Let 'em wait. You must see her before Herr Nirlanger comes home. He's due any minute. She looks like a girl. So young! And actually pretty! And her figure—divine! Funny what a difference a decent pair of corsets, and a gown, and some puffs will make, h'm?"

Frau Knapf was panting as I pulled her after me in swift eagerness. Between puffs she brought out exclamations of surprise and unbelief such as: "Unmoglich! (Puff! Puff!) Aber—

wunderbar! (Puff! Puff!)"

We stopped before Frau Nirlanger's door. I struck a dramatic pose. "Prepare!" I cried grandly, and threw open the door with a bang.

Crouched against the wall at a far corner of the room was Frau Nirlanger. Her hands were clasped over her breast and her eyes were dilated as though she had been running. In the center of the room stood Konrad Nirlanger, and on his oogly face was the very oogliest look that I have ever seen on a man. He glanced at us as we stood transfixed in the doorway, and laughed a short, sneering laugh that was like a stinging blow on the cheek.

"So!" he said; and I would not have believed that men really said "So!" in that way outside of a melodrama. "So! You are in the little surprise, yes? You carry your meddling outside of your newspaper work, eh? I leave behind me an old wife in the morning and in the evening, presto! I find a young bride. Wonderful!—but wonderful!" He laughed an unmusical and mirthless laugh.

"But—don't you like it?" I asked, like a simpleton.

Frau Nirlanger seemed to shrink before our very eyes, so that the pretty gown hung in limp folds about her.

I stared, fascinated, at Konrad Nirlanger's cruel face with its little eyes that were too close together and its chin that curved in below the mouth and out again so grotesquely.

"Like it?" sneered Konrad Nirlanger. "For a young girl, yes. But how useless, this belated trousseau. What a waste of good money! For see, a young wife I do not want. Young women one can have in plenty, always. But I have an old woman married, and for an old woman the gowns need be few—eh, Frau Orme? And you too, Frau Knapf?"

Frau Knapf, crimson and staring, was dumb. There came a little shivering moan from the figure crouched in the corner, and Frau Nirlanger, her face queerly withered and ashen, crumpled slowly in a little heap on the floor and buried her shamed head in her arms.

Konrad Nirlanger turned to his wife, the black look on his face growing blacker.

"Come, get up Anna," he ordered, in German. "These heroics become not a woman of your years. And too, you must not ruin the so costly gown that will be returned to-morrow."

Frau Nirlanger's white face was lifted from the shelter of her arms. The stricken look was still upon it, but there was no cowering in her attitude now. Slowly she rose to her feet. I had not realized that she was so tall.

"The gown does not go back," she said.

"So?" he snarled, with a savage note in his voice. "Now hear me. There shall be no more buying of gowns and fripperies. You hear? It is for the wife to come to the husband for the money; not for her to waste it wantonly on gowns, like a creature of the streets. You," his voice was an insult, "you, with your wrinkles and your faded eyes in a gown of—" he turned inquiringly toward me—"How does one call it, that color, Frau Orme?"

There came a blur of tears to my eyes. "It is called ashes of roses," I answered. "Ashes of roses."

Konrad Nirlanger threw back his head and laughed a laugh as stinging as a whip-lash. "Ashes of roses! So? It is well named. For my dear wife it is poetically fit, is it not so? For see, her roses are but withered ashes, eh Anna?"

Deliberately and in silence Anna Nirlanger walked to the mirror and stood there, gazing at the woman in the glass. There was something dreadful and portentous about the calm and studied deliberation with which she critically viewed that reflection. She lifted her arms slowly and patted into place the locks that had become disarranged, turning her head from side to side to study the effect. Then she took from a drawer the bit of chamois skin that I had given her, and passed it lightly over her eyelids and cheeks, humming softly to herself the while. No music ever sounded so uncanny to my ears. The woman before the mirror looked at the woman in the mirror with a long, steady, measuring look. Then, slowly and deliberately, the long graceful folds of her lovely gown trailing behind her, she walked over to where her frowning husband stood. So might a queen have walked, head held high, gaze steady. She stopped within half a foot of him, her eyes level with his. For a long half-minute they stood thus, the faded blue eyes of the wife gazing into the sullen black eyes of the husband, and his were the first to drop, for all the noble blood in Anna Nirlanger's veins, and all her long line of gently bred ancestors were coming to her aid in dealing with her middle-class husband.

"You forget," she said, very slowly and distinctly. "If this were Austria, instead of Amerika, you would not forget. In Austria people of your class do not speak in this manner to those of my caste."

"Unsinn!" laughed Konrad Nirlanger. "This is Amerika."

"Yes," said Anna Nirlanger, "this is Amerika. And in Amerika all things are different. I see now that my people knew of what they spoke when they called me mad to think of wedding a clod of the people, such as you."

For a moment I thought that he was going to strike her. I think he would have, if she had flinched. But she did not. Her head was held high, and her eyes did not waver.

"I married you for love. It is most comical, is it not? With you I thought I should find peace, and happiness and a re-birth of the intellect that was being smothered in the splendor and artificiality and the restrictions of my life there. Well, I was wrong. But wrong. Now hear me!" Her voice was tense with passion. "There will be gowns—as many and as rich as I choose. You have said many times that the ladies of Amerika you admire. And see! I shall be also one of those so-admired ladies. My money shall go for gowns! For hats! For trifles of lace and velvet and fur! You shall learn that it is not a peasant woman whom you have married. This is Amerika, the land of the free, my husband. And see! Who is more of Amerika than I? Who?"

She laughed a high little laugh and came over to me, taking my hands in her own.

"Dear girl, you must run quickly and dress. For this evening we go to the theater. Oh, but you must. There shall be no unpleasantness, that I promise. My husband accompanies us—with joy. Is it not so, Konrad? With joy? So!"

Wildly I longed to decline, but I dared not. So I only nodded, for fear of the great lump in my throat, and taking Frau Knapf's hand I turned and fled with her. Frau Knapf was muttering:

"Du Hund! Du unverschamter Hund du!" in good Billingsgate German, and wiping her eyes with her apron. And I dressed with trembling fingers because I dared not otherwise face the brave little Austrian, the plucky little aborigine who, with the donning of the new Amerikanische gown had acquired some real Amerikanisch nerve.

CHAPTER XI

VON GERHARD SPEAKS

Of Von Gerhard I had not had a glimpse since that evening of my hysterical outburst. On Christmas day there had come a box of roses so huge that I could not find vases enough to hold its contents, although I pressed into service everything from Mason jars from the kitchen to hand-painted atrocities from the parlor. After I had given posies to Frau Nirlanger, and fastened a rose in Frau Knapf's hard knob of hair, where it bobbed in ludicrous discomfort, I still had enough to fill the washbowl. My room looked like a grand opera star's boudoir when she is expecting the newspaper reporters. I reveled in the glowing fragrance of the blossoms and felt very eastern and luxurious and popular. It had been a busy, happy, work-filled week, in which I had had to snatch odd moments for the selecting of certain wonderful toys for the Spalpeens. There had been dolls and doll-clothes and a marvelous miniature kitchen for the practical and stolid Sheila, and ingenious bits of mechanism that did unbelievable things when wound up, for the clever, imaginative Hans. I was not to have the joy of seeing their wide-eyed delight, but I knew that there would follow certain laboriously scrawled letters, filled with topsy-turvy capitals and crazily leaning words of thanks to the doting old auntie who had been such good fun the summer before.

Boarding-house Christmases had become an old story.

I had learned to accept them, even to those obscure and foreign parts of turkey which are seen only on boarding-house plates, and which would be recognized nowhere else as belonging to that stately bird.

Christmas at Knapf's had been a happy surprise; a day of hearty good cheer and kindness. There had even been a Christmas tree, hung with stodgy German angels and Pfeffernuesse and pink-frosted cakes. I found myself the bewildered recipient of gifts from everyone—from the Knapfs, and the aborigines and even from one of the crushed-looking wives. The aborigine whom they called Fritz had presented me with a huge and imposing Lebkuchen, reposing in a box with frilled border, ornamented with quaint little red-and-green German figures in sugar, and labeled Nurnberg in stout letters, for it had come all the way from that kuchen-famous city. The Lebkuchen I placed on my mantel shelf as befitted so magnificent a work of art. It was quite too elaborate and imposing to be sent the way of ordinary food, although it had a certain tantalizingly spicy scent that tempted one to break off a corner here and there.

On the afternoon of Christmas day I sat down to thank Dr. von Gerhard for the flowers as prettily as might be. Also I asked his pardon, a thing not hard to do with the perfume of his roses filling the room.

"For you," I wrote, "who are so wise in the ways of those tricky things called nerves, must know that it was only a mild hysteria that made me say those most unladylike things. I have written Norah all about it. She has replied, advising me to stick to the good-fellow role but not to dress the part. So when next you see me I shall be a perfectly safe and sane comrade in petticoats. And I promise you—no more outbursts."

So it happened that on the afternoon of New Year's day Von Gerhard and I gravely wished one another many happy and impossible things for the coming year, looking fairly and squarely into each other's eyes as we did so.

"So," said Von Gerhard, as one who is satisfied. "The nerfs are steady to-day. What do you say to a brisk walk along the lake shore to put us in a New Year frame of mind, and then a supper down-town somewhere, with a toast to Max and Norah?"

"You've saved my life! Sit down here in the parlor and gaze at the crepe-paper oranges while I powder my nose and get into some street clothes. I have such a story to tell you! It has made me quite contented with my lot."

The story was that of the Nirlangers; and as we struggled against a brisk lake breeze I told it, and partly because of the breeze, and partly because of the story, there were tears in my eyes when I had finished. Von Gerhard stared at me, aghast.

"But you are—crying!" he marveled, watching a tear slide down my nose.

"I'm not," I retorted. "Anyway I know it. I think I may blubber if I choose to, mayn't I, as well as other women?"

"Blubber?" repeated Von Gerhard, he of the careful and cautious English. "But most certainly, if you wish. I had thought that newspaper women did not indulge in the luxury of tears."

"They don't—often. Haven't the time. If a woman reporter were to burst into tears every time she saw something to weep over she'd be going about with a red nose and puffy eyelids half the time. Scarcely a day passes that does not bring her face to face with human suffering in some form. Not only must she see these things, but she must write of them so that those who read can also see them. And just because she does not wail and tear her hair and faint she popularly is supposed to be a flinty, cigarette-smoking creature who rampages up and down the land, seeking whom she may rend with her pen and gazing, dry-eyed, upon scenes of horrid bloodshed."

"And yet the little domestic tragedy of the Nirlangers can bring tears to your eyes?"

"Oh, that was quite different. The case of the Nirlangers had nothing to do with Dawn O'Hara, newspaper reporter. It was just plain Dawn O'Hara, woman, who witnessed that little tragedy. Mein Himmel! Are all German husbands like that?"

"Not all. I have a very good friend named Max—"

"O, Max! Max is an angel husband. Fancy Max and Norah waxing tragic on the subject of a gown! Now you—"

"I? Come, you are sworn to good-fellowship. As one comrade to another, tell me, what sort of husband do you think I should make, eh? The boorish Nirlanger sort, or the charming Max variety. Come, tell me—you who always have seemed so—so damnably able to take care of yourself." His eyes were twinkling in the maddening way they had.

I looked out across the lake to where a line of white-caps was piling up formidably only to break in futile wrath against the solid wall of the shore. And there came over me an equally futile wrath; that savage, unreasoning instinct in women which prompts them to hurt those whom they love.

"Oh, you!" I began, with Von Gerhard's amused eyes laughing down upon me. "I should say that you would be more in the Nirlanger style, in your large, immovable, Germansure way. Not that you would stoop to wrangle about money or gowns, but that you would control those things. Your wife will be a placid, blond, rather plump German Fraulein, of excellent family and no imagination. Men of your type always select negative wives. Twenty years ago she would have run to bring you your Zeitung and your slippers. She would be that kind, if Zeitung-and-slipper husbands still were in existence. You will be fond of her, in a patronizing sort of way, and she will never know the difference between that and being loved, not having a great deal of imagination, as I have said before. And you will go on becoming more and more famous, and she will grow plumper and more placid, and less and less understanding of what those komisch medical journals have to say so often about her husband who is always discovering things. And you will live happily ever after—"

A hand gripped my shoulder. I looked up, startled, into two blue eyes blazing down into mine. Von Gerhard's face was a painful red. I think that the hand on my shoulder even shook me a little, there on that bleak and deserted lake drive. I tried to wrench my shoulder free with a jerk.

"You are hurting me!" I cried.

A quiver of pain passed over the face that I had thought so calmly unemotional. "You talk of hurts! You, who set out deliberately and maliciously to make me suffer! How dare you then talk to me like this! You stab with a hundred knives—you, who know how I—"

"I'm sorry," I put in, contritely. "Please don't be so dreadful about it. After all, you asked me, didn't you? Perhaps I've hurt your vanity. There, I didn't mean that, either. Oh, dear, let's talk about something impersonal. We get along wretchedly of late."

The angry red ebbed away from Von Gerhard's face. The blaze of wrath in his eyes gave way to a deeper, brighter light that held me fascinated, and there came to his lips a smile of rare sweetness. The hand that had grasped my shoulder slipped down, down, until it met my hand and gripped it.

"Na, 's ist schon recht, Kindchen. Those that we most care for we would hurt always. When I have told you of my love for you, although already you know it, then you will tell me. Hush! Do not deny this thing. There shall be no more lies between us. There shall be only the truth, and no more about plump, blonde German wives who run with Zeitung and slippers. After all, it is no secret. Three months ago I told Norah. It was not news to her. But she trusted me."

I felt my face to be as white and as tense as his own. "Norah—knows!"

"It is better to speak these things. Then there need be no shifting of the eyes, no evasive words, no tricks, no subterfuge."

We had faced about and were retracing our steps, past the rows of peculiarly home-like houses that line Milwaukee's magnificent lake shore. Windows were hung with holiday scarlet and holly, and here and there a face was visible at a window, looking out at the man and woman walking swiftly along the wind-swept heights that rose far above the lake.

A wretched revolt seized me as I gazed at the substantial comfort of those normal, happy homes.

"Why did you tell me! What good can that do? At least we

were make-believe friends before. Suppose I were to tell you that I care, then what."

"I do not ask you to tell me," Von Gerhard replied, quietly.

"You need not. You know. You knew long, long ago. You know I love the big quietness of you, and your sureness, and the German way you have of twisting your sentences about, and the steady grip of your great firm hands, and the rareness of your laugh, and the simplicity of you. Why I love the very cleanliness of your ruddy skin, and the way your hair grows away from your forehead, and your walk, and your voice and—Oh, what is the use of it all?"

"Just this, Dawn. The light of day sweetens all things. We have dragged this thing out into the sunlight, where, if it grows, it will grow sanely and healthily. It was but an ugly, distorted, unsightly thing, sending out pale unhealthy shoots in the dark, unwholesome cellars of our inner consciences. Norah's knowing was the cleanest, sweetest thing about it."

"How wonderfully you understand her, and how right you are! Her knowing seems to make it as it should be, doesn't it? I am braver already, for the knowledge of it. It shall make no difference between us?"

"There is no difference, Dawn," said he.

"No. It is only in the story-books that they sigh, and groan and utter silly nonsense. We are not like that. Perhaps, after a bit, you will meet some one you care for greatly—not plump, or blond, or German, perhaps, but still—"

"Doch you are flippant?"

"I must say those things to keep the tears back. You would not have me wailing here in the street. Tell me just one thing, and there shall be no more fluttering breaths and languishing looks. Tell me, when did you begin to care?"

We had reached Knapfs' door-step. The short winter day was already drawing to its close. In the half-light Von Gerhard's eyes glowed luminous.

"Since the day I first met you at Norah's," he said, simply.

I stared at him, aghast, my ever-present sense of humor struggling to the surface. "Not—not on that day when you came into the room where I sat in the chair by the window, with a flowered quilt humped about my shoulders! And a fever-sore twisting my mouth! And my complexion the color of cheese, and my hair plastered back from my forehead, and my eyes like boiled onions!"

"Thank God for your gift of laughter," Von Gerhard said, and took my hand in his for one brief moment before he turned and walked away.

Quite prosaically I opened the big front door at Knapfs' to find Herr Knapf standing in the hallway with his:

"Nabben', Frau Orme."

And there was the sane and soothing scent of Wienerschnitzel and spluttering things in the air. And I ran upstairs to my room and turned on all the lights and looked at the starry-eyed creature in the mirror. Then I took the biggest, newest photograph of Norah from the mantel and looked at her for a long, long minute, while she looked back at me in her brave true way.

"Thank you, dear," I said to her. "Thank you. Would you think me stagey and silly if I were to kiss you, just once, on your beautiful trusting eyes?"

A telephone bell tinkled downstairs and Herr Knapf stationed himself at the foot of the stairs and roared my name.

When I had picked up the receiver: "This is Ernst," said the voice at the other end of the wire. "I have just remembered that I had asked you down-town for supper."

"I would rather thank God fasting," I replied, very softly, and hung the receiver on its hook.

CHAPTER XII

BENNIE THE CONSOLER

In a corner of Frau Nirlanger's bedroom, sheltered from draughts and glaring light, is a little wooden bed, painted blue and ornamented with stout red roses that are faded by time and much abuse. Every evening at eight o'clock three anxious-browed women hold low-spoken conclave about the quaint old bed, while its occupant sleeps and smiles as he sleeps, and clasps to his breast a chewed-looking woolly dog. For a new joy has come to the sad little Frau Nirlanger, and I, quite by accident, was the cause of bringing it to her. The queer little blue bed, with its faded roses, was brought down from the attic by Frau Knapf, for she is one of the three foster mothers of the small occupant of the bed. The occupant of the bed is named Bennie, and a corporation formed for the purpose of bringing him up in the way he should go is composed of: Dawn O'Hara Orme, President and Distracted Guardian; Mrs. Konrad Nirlanger, Cuddler-in-chief and Authority on the Subject of Bennie's Bed-time; Mr. Blackie Griffith, Good Angel, General Cut-up and Monitor off'n Bennie's Neckties and Toys; Dr. Ernst von Gerhard, Chief Medical Adviser, and Sweller of the Exchequer, with the Privilege of Selecting All Candies. Members of the corporation meet with great frequency evenings and Sundays, much to the detriment of a certain Book-in-the-making with which Dawn O'Hara Orme was wont to struggle o' evenings.

Bennie had been one of those little tragedies that find their way into juvenile court. Bennie's story was common enough, but Bennie himself had been different. Ten minutes after his first appearance in the court room everyone, from the big, bald judge to the newest probation officer, had fallen in love with him. Somehow, you wanted to smooth the hair from his forehead, tip his pale little face upward, and very gently kiss his smooth, white brow. Which alone was enough to distinguish Bennie, for Juvenile court children, as a rule, are distinctly not kissable.

Bennie's mother was accused of being unfit to care for her boy, and Bennie was temporarily installed in the Detention Home. There the superintendent and his plump and kindly wife had fallen head over heels in love with him, and had dressed him in a smart little Norfolk suit and a frivolous plaid silk tie. There were delays in the case, and postponement after postponement, so that Bennie appeared in the court room every Tuesday for four weeks. The reporters, and the probation officers and policemen became very chummy with Bennie, and showered him with bright new pennies and certain wonderful candies. Superintendent Arnett of the Detention Home was as proud of the boy as though he were his own. And when Bennie would look shyly and questioningly into his face for permission to accept the proffered offerings, the big superintendent would chuckle delightedly. Bennie had a strangely mobile face for such a baby, and the whitest, smoothest brow I have ever seen.

The comedy and tears and misery and laughter of the big, white-walled court room were too much for Bennie. He would gaze about with puzzled blue eyes; then, giving up the situation as something too vast for his comprehension, he would fall to drawing curly-cues on a bit of paper with a great yellow pencil presented him by one of the newspaper men.

Every Tuesday the rows of benches were packed with a motley crowd of Poles, Russians, Slavs, Italians, Greeks, Lithuanians—a crowd made up of fathers, mothers, sisters, brothers, aunts, uncles, neighbors, friends, and enemies of the boys and girls whose fate was in the hands of the big man seated in the revolving chair up in front. But Bennie's mother was not of this crowd; this pitiful, ludicrous crowd filling the great room with the stifling, rancid odor of the poor. Nor was Bennie. He sat, clear-eyed and unsmiling, in the depths of a great chair on the court side of the railing and gravely received the attentions of the lawyers, and reporters and court room attaches who had grown fond of the grave little figure.

Then, on the fifth Tuesday, Bennie's mother appeared. How she had come to be that child's mother God only knows—or perhaps He had had nothing to do with it. She was terribly sober and frightened. Her face was swollen and bruised, and beneath one eye there was a puffy green-and-blue swelling. Her sordid story was common enough as the probation officer told it. The woman had been living in one wretched room with the boy. Her husband had deserted her. There was no food, and little furniture. The queer feature of it, said the probation officer, was that the woman managed to keep the boy fairly neat and clean, regardless of her own condition, and he generally had food of some sort, although the mother sometimes went without food for days. Through the squalor and misery and degradation of her own life Bennie had somehow been kept unsullied, a thing apart.

"H'm!" said judge Wheeling, and looked at Bennie. Bennie was standing beside his mother. He was very quiet, and his eyes were smiling up into those of the battered creature who was fighting for him. "I guess we'll have to take you out of this," the judge decided, abruptly. "That boy is too good to go to waste."

The sodden, dazed woman before him did not immediately get the full meaning of his words. She still stood there, swaying a bit, and staring unintelligently at the judge. Then, quite suddenly, she realized it. She took a quick step forward. Her hand went up to her breast, to her throat, to her lips, with an odd, stifled gesture.

"You ain't going to take him away! From me! No, you wouldn't do that, would you? Not for—not for always! You wouldn't do that—you wouldn't—"

Judge Wheeling waved her away. But the woman dropped to her knees.

"Judge, give me a chance! I'll stop drinking. Only don't take him away from me! Don't, judge, don't! He's all I've got in the world. Give me a chance. Three months! Six months! A year!"

"Get up!" ordered judge Wheeling, gruffly, "and stop that! It won't do you a bit of good."

And then a wonderful thing happened. The woman rose to her feet. A new and strange dignity had come into her battered face. The lines of suffering and vice were erased as by magic, and she seemed to grow taller, younger, almost beautiful. When she spoke again it was slowly and distinctly, her words quite free from the blur of the barroom and street vernacular.

"I tell you you must give me a chance. You cannot take a child from a mother in this way. I tell you, if you will only help me I can crawl back up the road that I've traveled. I was not always like this. There was another life, before—before—Oh, since then there have been years of blackness, and hunger, and cold and—worse! But I never dragged the boy into it. Look at him!"

Our eyes traveled from the woman's transfigured face to that of the boy. We could trace a wonderful likeness where before we had seen none. But the woman went on in her steady, even tone.

"I can't talk as I should, because my brain isn't clear. It's the drink. When you drink, you forget. But you must help me. I can't do it alone. I can remember how to live straight, just as I can remember how to talk straight. Let me show you that I'm not all bad. Give me a chance. Take the boy and then give him back to me when you are satisfied. I'll try—God only knows how I'll try. Only don't take him away forever, Judge! Don't do that!"

Judge Wheeling ran an uncomfortable finger around his collar's edge.

"Any friends living here?"

"No! No!"

"Sure about that?"

"Quite sure."

"Now see here; I'm going to give you your chance. I shall take this boy away from you for a year. In that time you will stop drinking and become a decent, self-supporting woman. You will be given in charge of one of these probation officers. She will find work for you, and a good home, and she'll stand by you, and you must report to her. If she is satisfied with you at the end of the year, the boy goes back to you."

"She will be satisfied," the woman said, simply. She stooped and taking Bennie's face between her hands kissed him once. Then she stepped aside and stood quite still, looking after the little figure that passed out of the court room with his hand in that of a big, kindly police officer. She looked until the big door had opened and closed upon them.

Then—well, it was just another newspaper story. It made a good one. That evening I told Frau Nirlanger about it, and she wept, softly, and murmured: "Ach, das arme baby! Like my little Oscar he is, without a mother." I told Ernst about him too, and Blackie, because I could not get his grave little face out of my mind. I wondered if those who had charge of him now would take the time to bathe the little body, and brush the soft hair until it shone, and tie the gay plaid silk tie as lovingly as "Daddy" Arnett of the Detention Home had done.

Then it was that I, quite unwittingly, stepped into Bennie's life.

There was an anniversary, or a change in the board of directors, or a new coat of paint or something of the kind in one of the orphan homes, and the story fell to me. I found the orphan home to be typical of its kind—a big, dreary, prison-like structure. The woman at the door did not in the least care to let me in. She was a fish-mouthed woman with a hard eye, and as I told my errand her mouth grew fishier and the eye harder. Finally she led me down a long, dark, airless stretch of corridor and departed in search of the matron, leaving me seated in the unfriendly reception room, with its straight-backed chairs placed stonily against the walls, beneath rows of red and blue and yellow religious pictures.

Just as I was wondering why it seemed impossible to be holy and cheerful at the same time, there came a pad-padding down the corridor. The next moment the matron stood in the doorway. She was a mountainous, red-faced woman, with warts on her nose.

"Good-afternoon," I said, sweetly. ("Ugh! What a brute!") I thought. Then I began to explain my errand once more. Criticism of the Home? No indeed, I assured her. At last, convinced of my disinterestedness she reluctantly guided me about the big, gloomy building. There were endless flights of shiny stairs, and endless stuffy, airless rooms, until we came to a door which she flung open, disclosing the nursery. It seemed to me that there were a hundred babies—babies at every stage of development, of all sizes, and ages and types. They glanced up at the opening of the door, and then a dreadful thing happened.

Every child that was able to walk or creep scuttled into the farthest corners and remained quite, quite still with a wide-eyed expression of fear and apprehension on every face.

For a moment my heart stood still. I turned to look at the woman by my side. Her thin lips were compressed into a straight, hard line. She said a word to a nurse standing near, and began to walk about, eying the children sharply. She put out a hand to pat the head of one red-haired mite in a soiled pinafore; but before her hand could descend I saw the child dodge and the tiny hand flew up to the head, as though in defense.

"They are afraid of her!" my sick heart told me. "Those babies are afraid of her! What does she do to them? I can't stand this. I'm going."

I mumbled a hurried "Thank you," to the fat matron as I turned to leave the big, bare room. At the head of the stairs there was a great, black door. I stopped before it—God knows why!—and pointed toward it.

"What is in that room?" I asked. Since then I have wondered many times at the unseen power that prompted me to put the question.

The stout matron bustled on, rattling her keys as she walked.

"That—oh, that's where we keep the incorrigibles."

"May I see them?" I asked, again prompted by that inner voice.

"There is only one." She grudgingly unlocked the door, using one of the great keys that swung from her waist. The heavy, black door swung open. I stepped into the bare room, lighted dimly by one small window. In the farthest corner crouched something that stirred and glanced up at our entrance. It peered at us with an ugly look of terror and defiance, and I stared back at it, in the dim light. During one dreadful, breathless second I remained staring, while my heart stood still. Then—"Bennie!" I cried. And stumbled toward him. "Bennie—boy!"

The little unkempt figure, in its soiled knickerbocker suit, the sunny hair all uncared for, the gay plaid tie draggled and limp, rushed into my arms with a crazy, inarticulate cry.

Down on my knees on the bare floor I held him close—close! and his arms were about my neck as though they never should unclasp.

"Take me away! Take me away!" His wet cheek was pressed against my own streaming one. "I want my mother! I want Daddy Arnett! Take me away!"

I wiped his cheeks with my notebook or something, picked him up in my arms, and started for the door. I had quite forgotten the fat matron.

"What are you doing?" she asked, blocking the doorway with her huge bulk.

"I'm going to take him back with me. Please let me! I'll take care of him until the year is up. He shan't bother you any more."

"That is impossible," she said, coldly. "He has been sent here by the court, for a year, and he must stay here. Besides, he is a stubborn, uncontrollable child."

"Uncontrollable! He's nothing of the kind! Why don't you treat him as a child should be treated, instead of like a little animal? You don't know him! Why, he's the most lovable—!

And he's only a baby! Can't you see that? A baby!"

She only stared her dislike, her little pig eyes grown smaller and more glittering.

"You great—big—thing!" I shrieked at her, like an infuriated child. With the tears streaming down my cheeks I unclasped Bennie's cold hands from about my neck. He clung to me, frantically, until I had to push him away and run.

The woman swung the door shut, and locked it. But for all its thickness I could hear Bennie's helpless fists pounding on its panels as I stumbled down the stairs, and Bennie's voice came faintly to my ears, muffled by the heavy door, as he shrieked to me to take him away to his mother, and to Daddy Arnett.

I blubbered all the way back in the car, until everyone stared, but I didn't care. When I reached the office I made straight for Blackie's smoke-filled sanctum. When my tale was ended he let me cry all over his desk, with my head buried in a heap of galley-proofs and my tears watering his paste-pot. He sat calmly by, smoking. Finally he began gently to philosophize. "Now girl, he's prob'ly better off there than he ever was at home with his mother soused all the time. Maybe he give that warty matron friend of yours all kinds of trouble, yellin' for his ma."

I raised my head from the desk. "Oh, you can talk! You didn't see him. What do you care! But if you could have seen him, crouched there—alone—like a little animal! He was so sweet—and lovable—and—and—he hadn't been decently washed for weeks—and his arms clung to me—I can feel his hands about my neck!—"

I buried my head in the papers again. Blackie went on smoking. There was no sound in the little room except the purr-purring of Blackie's pipe. Then:

"I done a favor for Wheeling once," mused he.

I glanced up, quickly. "Oh, Blackie, do you think—"

"No, I don't. But then again, you can't never tell. That was four or five years ago, and the mem'ry of past favors grows dim fast. Still, if you're through waterin' the top of my desk, why I'd like t' set down and do a little real brisk talkin' over the phone. You're excused."

Quite humbly I crept away, with hope in my heart.

To this day I do not know what secret string the resourceful Blackie pulled. But the next afternoon I found a hastily scrawled note tucked into the roll of my typewriter. It sent me scuttling across the hall to the sporting editor's smoke-filled room. And there on a chair beside the desk, surrounded by scrap-books, lead pencils, paste-pot and odds and ends of newspaper office paraphernalia, sat Bennie. His hair was parted very smoothly on one side, and under his dimpled chin bristled a very new and extremely lively green-and-red plaid silk tie.

The next instant I had swept aside papers, brushes, pencils, books, and Bennie was gathered close in my arms. Blackie, with a strange glow in his deep-set black eyes regarded us with an assumed disgust.

"Wimmin is all alike. Ain't it th' truth? I used t' think you was different. But shucks! It ain't so. Got t' turn on the weeps the minute you're tickled or mad. Why say, I ain't goin' t' have you comin' in here an' dampenin' up the whole place every little while! It's unhealthy for me, sittin' here in the wet."

"Oh, shut up, Blackie," I said, happily. "How in the world did you do it?"

"Never you mind. The question is, what you goin' t' do with him, now you've got him? Goin' t' have a French bunny for him, or fetch him up by hand? Wheeling appointed a probation skirt to look after the crowd of us, and we got t' toe the mark."

"Glory be!" I ejaculated. "I don't know what I shall do with him. I shall have to bring him down with me every morning, and perhaps you can make a sporting editor out of him."

"Nix. Not with that forehead. He's a high-brow. We'll make him dramatic critic. In the meantime, I'll be little fairy godmother, an' if you'll get on your bonnet I'll stake you and the young 'un to strawberry shortcake an' chocolate ice cream."

So it happened that a wondering Frau Knapf and a

sympathetic Frau Nirlanger were called in for consultation an hour later. Bennie was ensconced in my room, very wide-eyed and wondering, but quite content. With the entrance of Frau Nirlanger the consultation was somewhat disturbed. She made a quick rush at him and gathered him in her hungry arms.

"Du baby du!" she cried. "Du Kleiner! And she was down on her knees, and somehow her figure had melted into delicious mother-curves, with Bennie's head just fitting into that most gracious one between her shoulder and breast. She cooed to him in a babble of French and German and English, calling him her lee-tel Oscar. Bennie seemed miraculously to understand. Perhaps he was becoming accustomed to having strange ladies snatch him to their breasts.

"So," said Frau Nirlanger, looking up at us. "Is he not sweet? He shall be my lee-tel boy, nicht? For one small year he shall be my own boy. Ach, I am but lonely all the long day here in this strange land. You will let me care for him, nicht? And Konrad, he will be very angry, but that shall make no bit of difference. Eh, Oscar?"

And so the thing was settled, and an hour later three anxious-browed women were debating the weighty question of eggs or bread-and-milk for Bennie's supper. Frau Nirlanger was for soft-boiled eggs as being none too heavy after orphan asylum fare; I was for bread-and-milk, that being the prescribed supper dish for all the orphans and waifs that I had ever read about, from "The Wide, Wide World" to "Helen's Babies," and back again. Frau Knapf was for both eggs and bread-and-milk with a dash of meat and potatoes thrown in for good measure, and a slice or so of Kuchen on the side. We compromised on one egg, one glass of milk, and a slice of lavishly buttered bread, and jelly. It was a clean, sweet, sleepy-eyed Bennie that we tucked between the sheets. We three women stood looking down at him as he lay there in the quaint old blue-painted bed that had once held the plump little Knapfs.

"You think anyway he had enough supper? mused the

anxious-browed Frau Knapf.

"To school he will have to go, yes?" murmured Frau Nirlanger, regretfully.

I tucked in the covers at one side of the bed, not that they needed tucking, but because it was such a comfortable, satisfying thing to do.

"Just at this minute," I said, as I tucked, "I'd rather be a newspaper reporter than anything else in the world. As a profession 'tis so broadenin', an' at the same time, so chancey."

CHAPTER XIII

THE TEST

Some day the marriageable age for women will be advanced from twenty to thirty, and the old maid line will be changed from thirty to forty. When that time comes there will be surprisingly few divorces. The husband of whom we dream at twenty is not at all the type of man who attracts us at thirty. The man I married at twenty was a brilliant, morbid, handsome, abnormal creature with magnificent eyes and very white teeth and no particular appetite at mealtime. The man whom I could care for at thirty would be the normal, safe and substantial sort who would come in at six o'clock, kiss me once, sniff the air twice and say: "Mm! What's that smells so good, old girl? I'm as hungry as a bear. Trot it out. Where are the kids?"

These are dangerous things to think upon. So dangerous and disturbing to the peace of mind that I have decided not to see Ernst von Gerhard for a week or two. I find that seeing him is apt to make me forget Peter Orme; to forget that my duty begins with a capital D; to forget that I am dangerously near the thirty year old mark; to forget Norah, and Max, and the Spalpeens, and the world, and everything but the happiness of being near him, watching his eyes say one thing while his lips say another.

At such times I am apt to work myself up into rather a savage frame of mind, and to shut myself in my room evenings, paying no heed to Frau Nirlanger's timid knocking, or Bennie's good-night message. I uncover my typewriter and set to work at the thing which may or may not be a book, and am extremely wretched and gloomy and pessimistic, after this fashion:

"He probably wouldn't care anything about you if you were free. It is just a case of the fruit that is out of reach being the most desirable. Men don't marry frumpy, snuffy old things of thirty, or thereabouts. Men aren't marrying now-a-days, anyway. Certainly not for love. They marry for position, or power, or money, when they do marry. Think of all the glorious creatures he meets every day—women whose hair, and finger-nails and teeth and skin are a religion; women whose clothes are a fine art; women who are free to care only for themselves; to rest, to enjoy, to hear delightful music, and read charming books, and eat delicious food. He doesn't really care about you, with your rumpled blouses, and your shabby gloves and shoes, and your somewhat doubtful linen collars. The last time you saw him you were just coming home from the office after a dickens of a day, and there was a smudge on the end of your nose, and he told you of it, laughing. But you didn't laugh. You rubbed it off, furiously, and you wanted to cry. Cry! You, Dawn O'Hara! Begorra! 'Tis losin' your sense av humor you're after doin'! Get to work."

After which I would fall upon the book in a furious, futile fashion, writing many incoherent, irrelevant paragraphs which I knew would be cast aside as worthless on the sane and reasoning to-morrow.

Oh, it had been easy enough to talk of love in a lofty, superior impersonal way that New Year's day. Just the luxury of speaking of it at all, after those weeks of repression, sufficed. But it is not so easy to be impersonal and lofty when the touch of a coat sleeve against your arm sends little prickling, tingling shivers racing madly through thousands of too taut nerves. It is not so easy to force the mind and tongue into safe, sane channels when they are forever threatening to rush together in an overwhelming torrent that will carry misery and destruction in its wake. Invariably we talk with feverish earnestness about the book; about my work at the office; about Ernst's profession, with its wonderful growth; about Norah, and Max and the Spalpeens, and the home; about the latest news; about the weather; about

Peter Orme—and then silence.

At our last meeting things took a new and startling turn. So startling, so full of temptation and happiness-that-must-not-be, that I resolved to forbid myself the pain and joy of being, near him until I could be quite sure that my grip on Dawn O'Hara was firm, unshakable and lasting.

Von Gerhard sports a motor-car, a rakish little craft, built long and low, with racing lines, and a green complexion, and a nose that cuts through the air like the prow of a swift boat through water. Von Gerhard had promised me a spin in it on the first mild day. Sunday turned out to be unexpectedly lamblike, as only a March day can be, with real sunshine that warmed the end of one's nose instead of laughing as it tweaked it, as the lying February sunshine had done.

"But warmly you must dress yourself," Von Gerhard warned me, "with no gauzy blouses or sleeveless gowns. The air cuts like a knife, but it feels good against the face. And a little road-house I know, where one is served great steaming plates of hot oyster stew. How will that be for a lark, yes?"

And so I had swathed myself in wrappings until I could scarcely clamber into the panting little car, and we had darted off along the smooth lake drives, while the wind whipped the scarlet into our cheeks, even while it brought the tears to our eyes. There was no chance for conversation, even if Von Gerhard had been in talkative mood, which he was not. He seemed more taciturn than usual, seated there at the wheel, looking straight ahead at the ribbon of road, his eyes narrowed down to mere keen blue slits. I realized, without alarm, that he was driving furiously and lawlessly, and I did not care. Von Gerhard was that sort of man. One could sit quite calmly beside him while he pulled at the reins of a pair of runaway horses, knowing that he would conquer them in the end.

Just when my face began to feel as stiff and glazed as a mummy's, we swung off the roadway and up to the entrance of the road-house that was to revive us with things hot and soupy.

"Another minute," I said, through stiff lips, as I extricated myself from my swathings, "and I should have been what Mr. Mantalini described as a demnition body. For pity's sake, tell 'em the soup can't be too hot nor too steaming for your lady friend. I've had enough fresh air to last me the remainder of my life. May I timidly venture to suggest that a cheese sandwich follow the oyster stew? I am famished, and this place looks as though it might make a speciality of cheese sandwiches."

"By all means a cheese sandwich. Und was noch? That fresh air it has given you an appetite, nicht wahr?" But there was no sign of a smile on his face, nor was the kindly twinkle of amusement to be seen in his eyes—that twinkle that I had learned to look for.

"Smile for the lady," I mockingly begged when we had been served. "You've been owlish all the afternoon. Here, try a cheese sandwich. Now, why do you suppose that this mustard tastes so much better than the kind one gets at home?"

Von Gerhard had been smoking a cigarette, the first that I had ever seen in his fingers. Now he tossed it into the fireplace that yawned black and empty at one side of the room. He swept aside the plates and glasses that stood before him, leaned his arms on the table and deliberately stared at me.

"I sail for Europe in June, to be gone a year—probably more," he said.

"Sail!" I echoed, idiotically; and began blindly to dab clots of mustard on that ridiculous sandwich.

"I go to study and work with Gluck. It is the opportunity of a lifetime. Gluck is to the world of medicine what Edison is to the world of electricity. He is a wizard, a man inspired. You should see him—a little, bent, grizzled, shabby old man who looks at you, and sees you not. It is a wonderful opportunity, a—"

The mustard and the sandwich and the table and Von Gerhard's face were very indistinct and uncertain to my eyes, but I managed to say: "So glad—congratulate you—very happy—no doubt fortunate—"

Two strong hands grasped my wrists. "Drop that absurd mustard spoon and sandwich. Na, I did not mean to frighten you, Dawn. How your hands tremble. So, look at me. You would like Vienna, Kindchen. You would like the gayety, and the brightness of it, and the music, and the pretty women, and the incomparable gowns. Your sense of humor would discern the hollowness beneath all the pomp and ceremony and rigid lines of caste, and military glory; and your writer's instinct would revel in the splendor, and color and romance and intrigue."

I shrugged my shoulders in assumed indifference. "Can't you convey all this to me without grasping my wrists like a villain in a melodrama? Besides, it isn't very generous or thoughtful of you to tell me all this, knowing that it is not for me. Vienna for you, and Milwaukee and cheese sandwiches for me. Please pass the mustard."

But the hold on my wrists grew firmer. Von Gerhard's eyes were steady as they gazed into mine. "Dawn, Vienna, and the whole world is waiting for you, if you will but take it. Vienna—and happiness—with me—"

I wrenched my wrists free with a dreadful effort and rose, sick, bewildered, stunned. My world—my refuge of truth, and honor, and safety and sanity that had lain in Ernst von Gerhard's great, steady hands, was slipping away from me. I think the horror that I felt within must have leaped to my eyes, for in an instant Von Gerhard was beside me, steadying me with his clear blue eyes. He did not touch the tips of my fingers as he stood there very near me. From the look of pain on his face I knew that I had misunderstood, somehow.

"Kleine, I see that you know me not," he said, in German, and the saying it was as tender as is a mother when she reproves a child that she loves. "This fight against the world, those years of unhappiness and misery, they have made you suspicious and lacking in trust, is it not so? You do not yet know the perfect love that casts out all doubt. Dawn, I ask you in the name of all that is reasoning, and for the sake of your happiness and mine, to divorce this man Peter Orme—this man who for almost ten years has not been your husband—who never can be your husband. I ask you to do something which will bring suffering to no one, and which will mean happiness to many. Let me make you happy—you were born to be happy—you who can laugh like a girl in spite of your woman's sorrows—"

But I sank into a chair and hid my face in my hands so that I might be spared the beauty and the tenderness of his eyes. I tried to think of all the sane and commonplace things in life. Somewhere in my inner consciousness a cool little voice was saying, over and over again:

"Now, Dawn, careful! You've come to the crossroads at last. Right or left? Choose! Now, Dawn, careful!" and the rest of it all over again.

When I lifted my face from my hands at last it was to meet the tenderness of Von Gerhard's gaze with scarcely a tremor.

"You ought to know," I said, very slowly and evenly, "that a divorce, under these circumstances, is almost impossible, even if I wished to do what you suggest. There are certain state laws—"

An exclamation of impatience broke from him. "Laws! In some states, yes. In others, no. It is a mere technicality—a trifle! There is about it a bit of that which you call red tape. It amounts to nothing—to that!" He snapped his fingers. "A few months' residence in another state, perhaps. These American laws, they are made to break."

"Yes; you are quite right," I said, and I knew in my heart that the cool, insistent little voice within had not spoken in vain. "But there are other laws—laws of honor and decency, and right living and conscience—that cannot be broken with such ease. I cannot marry you. I have a husband."

"You can call that unfortunate wretch your husband! He does not know that he has a wife. He will not know that he has lost a wife. Come, Dawn—small one—be not so foolish. You do not know how happy I will make you. You have never seen me except when I was tortured with doubts and fears. You do not know what our life will be together. There shall be everything to make you forget—everything that thought and love and money can give you. The man there in the barred room—"

At that I took his dear hands in mine and held them close as I miserably tried to make him hear what that small, still voice had told me.

"There! That is it! If he were free, if he were able to stand before men that his actions might be judged fairly and justly, I should not hesitate for one single, precious moment. If he could fight for his rights, or relinquish them, as he saw fit, then this thing would not be so monstrous. But, Ernst, can't you see? He is there, alone, in that dreadful place, quite helpless, quite incapable, quite at our mercy. I should as soon think of hurting a little child, or snatching the pennies from a blind man's cup. The thing is inhuman! It is monstrous! No state laws, no red tape can dissolve such a union."

"You still care for him!"

"Ernst!"

His face was very white with the pallor of repressed emotion, and his eyes were like the blue flame that one sees flashing above a bed of white-hot coals.

"You do care for him still. But yes! You can stand there, quite cool—but quite—and tell me that you would not hurt him, not for your happiness, not for mine. But me you can hurt again and again, without one twinge of regret."

There was silence for a moment in the little bare dining-room—a miserable silence on my part, a bitter one for Ernst. Then Von Gerhard seated himself again at the table opposite and smiled one of the rare smiles that illumined his face with such sweetness.

"Come, Dawn, almost we are quarreling—we who were to have been so matter-of-fact and sensible. Let us make an end of this question. You will think of what I have said, will you not? Perhaps I was too abrupt, too brutal. Ach, Dawn, you know not how I—Very well, I will not."

With both hands I was clinging to my courage and praying for strength to endure this until I should be alone in my room again.

"As for that poor creature who is bereft of reason, he shall lack no care, no attention. The burden you have borne so long I shall take now upon my shoulders."

He seemed so confident, so sure. I could bear it no longer. "Ernst, if you have any pity, any love for me, stop! I tell you I can never do this. Why do you make it so terribly hard for me! So pitilessly hard! You always have been so strong, so sure, such a staff of courage."

"I say again, and again, and again, you do not care."

It was then that I took my last vestige of strength and courage together and going over to him, put my two hands on his great shoulders, looking up into his drawn face as I spoke.

"Ernst, look at me! You never can know how much I care. I care so much that I could not bear to have the shadow of wrong fall upon our happiness. There can be no lasting happiness upon a foundation of shameful deceit. I should hate myself, and you would grow to hate me. It always is so. Dear one, I care so much that I have the strength to do as I would do if I had to face my mother, and Norah tonight. I don't ask you to understand. Men are not made to understand these things; not even a man such as you, who are so beautifully understanding. I only ask that you believe in me—and think of me sometimes—I shall feel it, and be helped. Will you take me home now, Dr. von Gerhard?"

The ride home was made in silence. The wind was colder, sharper. I was chilled, miserable, sick. Von Gerhard's face was quite expressionless as he guided the little car over the smooth road. When we had stopped before my door, still without a word, I thought that he was going to leave me with that barrier of silence unbroken. But as I stepped stiffly to the curbing his hands closed about mine with the old steady grip. I looked up quickly, to find a smile in the corners of the tired eyes.

"You—you will let me see you—sometimes?"

But wisdom came to my aid. "Not now. It is better that we go our separate ways for a few weeks, until our work has served to adjust the balance that has been disturbed. At the end of that time I shall write you, and from that time until you sail in June we shall be just good comrades again. And once in Vienna—who knows?—you may meet the plump blond Fraulein, of excellent family—"

"And no particular imagination—"

And then we both laughed, a bit hysterically, because laughter is, after all, akin to tears. And the little green car shot off with a whir as I turned to enter my new world of loneliness.

CHAPTER XIV

BENNIE AND THE CHARMING OLD MAID

There followed a blessed week of work—a "human warious" week, with something piquant lurking at every turn. A week so busy, so kaleidoscopic in its quick succession of events that my own troubles and grievances were pushed into a neglected corner of my mind and made to languish there, unfed by tears or sighs.

News comes in cycles. There are weeks when a city editor tears his hair in vain as he bellows for a first-page story. There follow days so bristling with real, live copy that perfectly good stuff which, in the ordinary course of events might be used to grace the front sheet, is sandwiched away between the marine intelligence and the Elgin butter reports.

Such a week was this. I interviewed everything from a red-handed murderer to an incubator baby. The town seemed to be running over with celebrities. Norberg, the city editor, adores celebrities. He never allows one to escape uninterviewed. On Friday there fell to my lot a world-famous prima donna, an infamous prize-fighter, and a charming old maid. Norberg cared not whether the celebrity in question was noted for a magnificent high C, or a left half-scissors hook, so long as the interview was dished up hot and juicy, with plenty of quotation marks, a liberal sprinkling of adjectives and adverbs, and a cut of the victim gracing the top of the column.

It was long past the lunch hour when the prima donna and the prize-fighter, properly embellished, were snapped on the copy hook. The prima donna had chattered in French; the prize-fighter had jabbered in slang; but the charming old maid, who spoke Milwaukee English, was to make better copy than a whole chorus of prima donnas, or a ring full of fighters. Copy! It was such wonderful stuff that I couldn't use it.

It was with the charming old maid in mind that Norberg summoned me.

"Another special story for you," he cheerfully announced.

No answering cheer appeared upon my lunchless features. "A prize-fighter at ten-thirty, and a prima donna at twelve. What's the next choice morsel? An aeronaut with another successful airship? or a cash girl who has inherited a million?"

Norberg's plump cheeks dimpled. "Neither. This time it is a nice German old maid."

"Eloped with the coachman, no doubt?"

"I said a nice old maid. And she hasn't done anything yet. You are to find out how she'll feel when she does it."

"Charmingly lucid," commented I, made savage by the pangs of hunger.

Norberg proceeded to outline the story with characteristic vigor, a cigarette waggling from the corner of his mouth.

"Name and address on this slip. Take a Greenfield car. Nice old maid has lived in nice old cottage all her life. Grandfather built it himself about a hundred years ago. Whole family was born in it, and married in it, and died in it, see? It's crammed full of spinning-wheels and mahogany and stuff that'll make your eyes stick out. See? Well, there's no one left now but the nice old maid, all alone. She had a sister who ran away with a scamp some years ago. Nice old maid has never heard of her since, but she leaves the gate ajar or the latch-string open, or a lamp in the window, or something, so that if ever she wanders back to the old home she'll know she's welcome, see?"

"Sounds like a moving picture play," I remarked.

"Wait a minute. Here's the point. The city wants to build a branch library or something on her property, and the nice old party is so pinched for money that she'll have to take their offer. So the time has come when she'll have to leave that old cottage, with its romance, and its memories, and its lamp in the window, and go to live in a cheap little flat, see? Where the old four-poster will choke up the bedroom—"

"And the parlor will be done in red and green," I put in, eagerly, "and where there will be an ingrowing sideboard in the dining-room that won't fit in with the quaint old dinner-set at all, and a kitchenette just off that, in which the great iron pots and kettles that used to hold the family dinners will be monstrously out of place—"

"You're on," said Norberg.

Half an hour later I stood before the cottage, set primly in the center of a great lot that extended for half a square on all sides. A winter-sodden, bare enough sight it was in the gray of that March day. But it was not long before Alma Pflugel, standing in the midst of it, the March winds flapping her neat skirts about her ankles, filled it with a blaze of color. As she talked, a row of stately hollyhocks, pink, and scarlet, and saffron, reared their heads against the cottage sides. The chill March air became sweet with the scent of heliotrope, and Sweet William, and pansies, and bridal wreath. The naked twigs of the rose bushes flowered into wondrous bloom so that they bent to the ground with their weight of crimson and yellow glory. The bare brick paths were overrun with the green of growing things. Gray mounds of dirt grew vivid with the fire of poppies. Even the rain-soaked wood of the pea-frames miraculously was hidden in a hedge of green, over which ran riot the butterfly beauty of the lavender, and pink, and cerise blossoms. Oh, she did marvelous things that dull March day, did plain German Alma Pflugel! And still more marvelous were the things that were to come.

But of these things we knew nothing as the door was opened and Alma Pflugel and I gazed curiously at one another. Surprise was writ large on her honest face as I disclosed my errand. It was plain that the ways of newspaper reporters were foreign to the life of this plain German woman, but she bade me enter with a sweet graciousness of manner.

Wondering, but silent, she led the way down the dim narrow hallway to the sitting-room beyond. And there I saw that Norberg had known whereof he spoke.

A stout, red-faced stove glowed cheerfully in one corner of the room. Back of the stove a sleepy cat opened one indolent eye, yawned shamelessly, and rose to investigate, as is the way of cats. The windows were aglow with the sturdy potted plants that flower-loving German women coax into bloom. The low-ceilinged room twinkled and shone as the polished surfaces of tables and chairs reflected the rosy glow from the plethoric stove. I sank into the depths of a huge rocker that must have been built for Grosspapa Pflugel's generous curves. Alma Pflugel, in a chair opposite, politely waited for this new process of interviewing to begin, but relaxed in the embrace of that great armchair I suddenly realized that I was very tired and hungry, and talk-weary, and that here; was a great peace. The prima donna, with her French, and her paint, and her pearls, and the prizefighter with his slang, and his cauliflower ear, and his diamonds, seemed creatures of another planet. My eyes closed. A delicious sensation of warmth and drowsy contentment stole over me.

"Do listen to the purring of that cat!" I murmured. "Oh, newspapers have no place in this. This is peace and rest."

Alma Pflugel leaned forward in her chair. "You—you like it?"

"Like it! This is home. I feel as though my mother were here in this room, seated in one of those deep chairs, with a bit of sewing in her hand; so near that I could touch her cheek with my fingers."

Alma Pflugel rose from her chair and came over to me. She timidly placed her hand on my arm. "Ah, I am so glad you are like that. You do not laugh at the low ceilings, and the sunken floors, and the old-fashioned rooms. You do not raise your eyes in horror and say: 'No conveniences! And why don't you try striped wall paper? It would make those dreadful ceilings seem higher.' How nice you are to understand like that!"

My hand crept over to cover her own that lay on my arm.

"Indeed, indeed I do understand," I whispered. Which, as the veriest cub reporter can testify, is no way to begin an interview.

A hundred happy memories filled the little low room as Alma Pflugel showed me her treasures. The cat purred in great content, and the stove cast a rosy glow over the scene as the simple woman told the story of each precious relic, from the battered candle-dipper on the shelf, to the great mahogany folding table, and sewing stand, and carved bed. Then there was the old horn lantern that Jacob Pflugel had used a century before, and in one corner of the sitting-room stood Grossmutter Pflugel's spinning-wheel. Behind cupboard doors were ranged the carefully preserved blue-and-white china dishes, and on the shelf below stood the clumsy earthen set that Grosspapa Pflugel himself had modeled for his young bride in those days of long ago. In the linen chest there still lay, in neat, fragrant folds, piles of the linen that had been spun on that time-yellowed spinning-wheel. And because of the tragedy in the honest face bent over these dear treasures, and because she tried so bravely to hide her tears, I knew in my heart that this could never be a newspaper story.

"So," said Alma Pflugel at last, and rose and walked slowly to the window and stood looking out at the wind-swept garden. That window, with its many tiny panes, once had looked out across a wilderness, with an Indian camp not far away. Grossmutter Pflugel had sat at that window many a bitter winter night, with her baby in her arms, watching and waiting for the young husband who was urging his ox-team across the ice of Lake Michigan in the teeth of a raging blizzard.

The little, low-ceilinged room was very still. I looked at Alma Pflugel standing there at the window in her neat blue gown, and something about the face and figure—or was it the pose of the sorrowful head?—seemed strangely familiar. Somewhere in my mind the resemblance haunted me. Resemblance to—what? Whom?

"Would you like to see my garden?" asked Alma Pflugel, turning from the window. For a moment I stared in wonderment.

But the honest, kindly face was unsmiling. "These things that I have shown you, I can take with me when I—go. But there," and she pointed out over the bare, wind-swept lot, "there is something that I cannot take. My flowers! You see that mound over there, covered so snug and warm with burlap and sacking? There my tulips and hyacinths sleep. In a few weeks, when the covering is whisked off—ah, you shall see! Then one can be quite sure that the spring is here. Who can look at a great bed of red and pink and lavender and yellow tulips and hyacinths, and doubt it? Come."

With a quick gesture she threw a shawl over her head, and beckoned me. Together we stepped out into the chill of the raw March afternoon. She stood a moment, silent, gazing over the sodden earth. Then she flitted swiftly down the narrow path, and halted before a queer little structure of brick, covered with the skeleton of a creeping vine. Stooping, Alma Pflugel pulled open the rusty iron door and smiled up at me.

"This was my grandmother's oven. All her bread she baked in this little brick stove. Black bread it was, with a great thick crust, and a bitter taste. But it was sweet, too. I have never tasted any so good. I like to think of Grossmutter, when she was a bride, baking her first batch of bread in this oven that Grossvater built for her. And because the old oven was so very difficult to manage, and because she was such a young thing—only sixteen!—I like to think that her first loaves were perhaps not so successful, and that Grosspapa joked about them, and that the little bride wept, so that the young husband had to kiss away the tears."

She shut the rusty, sagging door very slowly and gently. "No doubt the workmen who will come to prepare the ground for the new library will laugh and joke among themselves when they see the oven, and they will kick it with their heels, and wonder what the old brick mound could have been."

There was a little twisted smile on her face as she rose—a smile that brought a hot mist of tears to my eyes. There was tragedy itself in that spare, homely figure standing there in the garden, the wind twining her skirts about her.

"You should but see the children peering over the fence to see my flowers in the summer," she said. The blue eyes wore a wistful, far-away look. "All the children know my garden. It blooms from April to October. There I have my sweet peas; and here my roses—thousands of them! Some are as red as a drop of blood, and some as white as a bridal wreath. When they are blossoming it makes the heart ache, it is so beautiful."

She had quite forgotten me now. For her the garden was all abloom once more. It was as though the Spirit of the Flowers had touched the naked twigs with fairy fingers, waking them into glowing life for her who never again was to shower her love and care upon them.

"These are my poppies. Did you ever come out in the morning to find a hundred poppy faces smiling at you, and swaying and glistening and rippling in the breeze? There they are, scarlet and pink, side by side as only God can place them. And near the poppies I planted my pansies, because each is a lesson to the other. I call my pansies little children with happy faces. See how this great purple one winks his yellow eye, and laughs!"

Her gray shawl had slipped back from her face and lay about her shoulders, and the wind had tossed her hair into a soft fluff about her head.

"We used to come out here in the early morning, my little Schwester and I, to see which rose had unfolded its petals overnight, or whether this great peony that had held its white head so high only yesterday, was humbled to the ground in a heap of ragged leaves. Oh, in the morning she loved it best. And so every summer I have made the garden bloom again, so that when she comes back she will see flowers greet her.

"All the way up the path to the door she will walk in an aisle of fragrance, and when she turns the handle of the old door she will find it unlocked, summer and winter, day and night, so that she has only to turn the knob and enter."

She stopped, abruptly. The light died out of her face. She

glanced at me, half defiantly, half timidly, as one who is not quite sure of what she has said. At that I went over to her, and took her work-worn hands in mine, and smiled down into the faded blue eyes grown dim with tears and watching.

"Perhaps—who knows?—the little sister may come yet. I feel it. She will walk up the little path, and try the handle of the door, and it will turn beneath her fingers, and she will enter."

With my arm about her we walked down the path toward the old-fashioned arbor, bare now except for the tendrils that twined about the lattice. The arbor was fitted with a wooden floor, and there were rustic chairs, and a table. I could picture the sisters sitting there with their sewing during the long, peaceful summer afternoons. Alma Pflugel would be wearing one of her neat gingham gowns, very starched and stiff, with perhaps a snowy apron edged with a border of heavy crochet done by the wrinkled fingers of Grossmutter Pflugel. On the rustic table there would be a bowl of flowers, and a pot of delicious Kaffee, and a plate of German Kaffeekuchen, and through the leafy doorway the scent of the wonderful garden would come stealing.

I thought of the cheap little flat, with the ugly sideboard, and the bit of weedy yard in the rear, and the alley beyond that, and the red and green wall paper in the parlor. The next moment, to my horror, Alma Pflugel had dropped to her knees before the table in the damp little arbor, her face in her hands, her spare shoulders shaking.

"Ich kann's nicht thun!" she moaned. "Ich kann nicht! Ach, kleine Schwester, wo bist du denn! Nachts und Morgens bete ich, aber doch kommst du nicht."

A great dry sob shook her. Her hand went to her breast, to her throat, to her lips, with an odd, stifled gesture.

"Do that again!" I cried, and shook Alma Pflugel sharply by the shoulder. "Do that again!"

Her startled blue eyes looked into mine. "What do you mean?" she asked.

"That—that gesture. I've seen it—somewhere—that trick of

pressing the hand to the breast, to the throat, to the lips—Oh!"

Suddenly I knew. I lifted the drooping head and rumpled its neat braids, and laughed down into the startled face.

"She's here!" I shouted, and started a dance of triumph on the shaky floor of the old arbor. "I know her. From the moment I saw you the resemblance haunted me." And then as Alma Pflugel continued to stare, while the stunned bewilderment grew in her eyes, "Why, I have one-fourth interest in your own nephew this very minute. And his name is Bennie!"

Whereupon Alma Pflugel fainted quietly away in the chilly little grape arbor, with her head on my shoulder.

I called myself savage names as I chafed her hands and did all the foolish, futile things that distracted humans think of at such times, wondering, meanwhile, if I had been quite mad to discern a resemblance between this simple, clear-eyed gentle German woman, and the battered, ragged, swaying figure that had stood at the judge's bench.

Suddenly Alma Pflugel opened her eyes. Recognition dawned in them slowly. Then, with a jerk, she sat upright, her trembling hands clinging to me.

"Where is she? Take me to her. Ach, you are sure—sure?"

"Lordy, I hope so! Come, you must let me help you into the house. And where is the nearest telephone? Never mind; I'll find one."

When I had succeeded in finding the nearest drug store I spent a wild ten minutes telephoning the surprised little probation officer, then Frau Nirlanger, and finally Blackie, for no particular reason. I shrieked my story over the wire in disconnected, incoherent sentences. Then I rushed back to the little cottage where Alma Pflugel and I waited with what patience we could summon.

Blackie was the first to arrive. He required few explanations. That is one of the nicest things about Blackie. He understands by leaps and bounds, while others crawl to comprehension. But when Frau Nirlanger came, with Bennie in tow, there were tears, and exclamations, followed by a little stricken silence on the part of Frau Nirlanger when she saw Bennie snatched to the breast of this weeping woman. So it was that in the midst of the confusion we did not hear the approach of the probation officer and her charge. They came up the path to the door, and there the little sister turned the knob, and it yielded under her fingers, and the old door swung open; and so she entered the house quite as Alma Pflugel had planned she should, except that the roses were not blooming along the edge of the sunken brick walk.

She entered the room in silence, and no one could have recognized in this pretty, fragile creature the pitiful wreck of the juvenile court. And when Alma Pflugel saw the face of the little sister—the poor, marred, stricken face—her own face became terrible in its agony. She put Bennie down very gently, rose, and took the shaking little figure in her strong arms, and held it as though never to let it go again. There were little broken words of love and pity. She called her "Lammchen" and "little one," and so Frau Nirlanger and Blackie and I stole away, after a whispered consultation with the little probation officer.

Blackie had come in his red runabout, and now he tucked us into it, feigning a deep disgust.

"I'd like to know where I enter into this little drayma," he growled. "Ain't I got nothin' t' do but run around town unitin' long lost sisters an' orphans!"

"Now, Blackie, you know you would never have forgiven me if I had left you out of this. Besides, you must hustle around and see that they need not move out of that dear little cottage. Now don't say a word! You'll never have a greater chance to act the fairy godmother."

Frau Nirlanger's hand sought mine and I squeezed it in silent sympathy. Poor little Frau Nirlanger, the happiness of another had brought her only sorrow. And she had kissed Bennie good-by with the knowledge that the little blue-painted bed, with its faded red roses, would again stand empty in the gloom of the Knapf attic.

Norberg glanced up quickly as I entered the city room. "Get something good on that south side story?" he asked.

"Why, no," I answered. "You were mistaken about that. The—the nice old maid is not going to move, after all."

CHAPTER XV

FAREWELL TO KNAPFS

Consternation has corrugated the brows of the aborigines. Consternation twice confounded had added a wrinkle or two to my collection. We are homeless. That is, we are Knapfless—we, to whom the Knapfs spelled home.

Herr Knapf, mustache aquiver, and Frau Knapf, cheek bones glistening, broke the news to us one evening just a week after the exciting day which so changed Bennie's life. "Es thut uns sehr, sehr leid," Herr Knapf had begun. And before he had finished, protesting German groans mingled with voluble German explanations. The aborigines were stricken down. They clapped pudgy fists to knobby foreheads; they smote their breasts, and made wild gestures with their arms. If my protests were less frenzied than theirs, it was only because my knowledge of German stops at words of six syllables.

Out of the chaos of ejaculations and interrogation the reason for our expulsion at last was made clear. The little German hotel had not been remunerative. Our host and hostess were too hospitable and too polite to state the true reason for this state of affairs. Perhaps rents were too high. Perhaps, thought I, Frau Knapf had been too liberal with the butter in the stewed chicken. Perhaps there had been too many golden Pfannkuchen with real eggs and milk stirred into them, and with toothsome little islands of ruddy currant jelly on top. Perhaps there had been too much honest, nourishing food, and not enough boarding-house victuals. At any rate, the enterprise would have to be abandoned.

It was then that the bare, bright little dining room, with its queer prints of chin-chucking lieutenants, and its queerer faces, and its German cookery became very dear to me. I had grown to like Frau Knapf, of the shining cheek bones, and Herr Knapf, of the heavy geniality. A close bond of friendship had sprung up between Frau Nirlanger and me. I would miss her friendly visits, and her pretty ways, and her sparkling conversation. She and I had held many kimonoed pow-wows, and sometimes—not often—she had given me wonderful glimpses of that which she had left—of Vienna, the opera, the court, the life which had been hers. She talked marvelously well, for she had all the charm and vivacity of the true Viennese. Even the aborigines, bristling pompadours, thick spectacles, terrifying manner, and all, became as dear as old friends, now that I knew I must lose them.

The great, high-ceilinged room upstairs had taken on the look of home. The Blue-beard closet no longer appalled me. The very purpleness of the purple roses in the rug had grown beautiful in my eyes because they were part of that little domain which spelled peace and comfort and kindness. How could I live without the stout yellow brocade armchair! Its plethoric curves were balm for my tired bones. Its great lap admitted of sitting with knees crossed, Turk-fashion. Its cushioned back stopped just at the point where the head found needed support. Its pudgy arms offered rest for tired elbows; its yielding bosom was made for tired backs. Given the padded comfort of that stout old chair—a friendly, time-tried book between my fingers—a dish of ruddy apples twinkling in the fire-light; my mundane soul snuggled in content. And then, too, the book-in-the-making had grown in that room. It had developed from a weak, wobbling uncertainty into a lusty full-blooded thing that grew and grew until it promised soon to become mansize.

Now all this was to be changed. And I knew that I would miss the easy German atmosphere of the place; the kindness they had shown me; the chattering, admiring Minna; the taffy-colored dachshund; the aborigines with their ill-smelling pipes and flappy slippers; the Wienerschnitzel; the crushed-looking wives and the masterful German husbands; the very darns in the table-cloths and the very nicks in the china.

We had a last family gathering in token of our appreciation of Herr and Frau Knapf. And because I had not seen him for almost three weeks; and because the time for his going was drawing so sickeningly near; and because I was quite sure that I had myself in hand; and because he knew the Knapfs, and was fond of them; and because-well, I invited Von Gerhard. He came, and I found myself dangerously glad to see him, so that I made my greeting as airy and frivolous as possible. Perhaps I overdid the airy business, for Von Gerhard looked at me for a long, silent minute, until the nonsense I had been chattering died on my lips, and I found myself staring up at him like a child that is apprehensive of being scolded for some naughtiness.

"Not so much chatter, small one," he said, unsmilingly. "This pretense, it is not necessary between you and me. So. You are ein bischen blasz, nicht? A little pale? You have not been ill, Dawn?"

"Ill? Never felt more chipper in my life," I made flippant answer, "and I adore these people who are forever telling one how unusually thin, or pale, or scrawny one is looking."

"Na, they are not to be satisfied, these women! If I were to tell you how lovely you look to me to-night you would draw yourself up with chill dignity and remind me that I am not privileged to say these things to you. So I discreetly mention that you are looking, interestingly pale, taking care to keep all tenderness out of my tones, and still you are not pleased." He shrugged despairing shoulders.

"Can't you strike a happy medium between rudeness and tenderness? After all, I haven't had a glimpse of your blond beauty for three weeks. And while I don't ask you to whisper sweet nothings, still, after twenty-one days—"

"You have been lonely? If only I thought that those weeks have been as wearisome to you—"

"Not lonely exactly," I hurriedly interrupted, "but sort of wishing that some one would pat me on the head and tell me that I was a good doggie. You know what I mean. It is so easy to become accustomed to thoughtfulness and devotion, and so dreadfully hard to be happy without it, once one has had it. This has been a sort of training for what I may expect when Vienna has swallowed you up."

"You are still obstinate? These three weeks have not changed you? Ach, Dawn! Kindchen!—"

But I knew that these were thin spots marked "Danger!" in our conversational pond. So, "Come," said I. "I have two new aborigines for you to meet. They are the very shiniest and wildest of all our shiny-faced and wild aborigines. And you should see their trousers and neckties! If you dare to come back from Vienna wearing trousers like these!—"

"And is the party in honor of these new aborigines?" laughed Von Gerhard. "You did not explain in your note. Merely you asked me to come, knowing that I cared not if it were a lawn fete or a ball, so long as I might again be with you."

We were on our way to the dining room, where the festivities were to be held. I stopped and turned a look of surprise upon him.

"Don't you know that the Knapfs are leaving? Did I neglect to mention that this is a farewell party for Herr and Frau Knapf? We are losing our home, and we have just one week in which to find another."

"But where will you go? And why did you not tell me this before?"

"I haven't an idea where I shall lay my poor old head. In the lap of the gods, probably, for I don't know how I shall find the time to interview landladies and pack my belongings in seven short days. The book will have to suffer for it. Just when it was getting along so beautifully, too."

There was a dangerous tenderness in Von Gerhard's eyes as he said: "Again you are a wanderer, eh—small one? That you, with your love of beautiful things, and your fastidiousness, should have to live in this way—in these boarding-houses, alone, with not even the comforts that should be yours. Ach, Kindchen, you were not made for that. You were intended for the home, with a husband, and kinder, and all that is truly worth while."

I swallowed a lump in my throat as I shrugged my shoulders. "Pooh! Any woman can have a husband and babies," I retorted, wickedly. "But mighty few women can write a book. It's a special curse."

"And you prefer this life—this existence, to the things that I offer you! You would endure these hardships rather than give up the nonsensical views which you entertain toward your—"

"Please. We were not to talk of that. I am enduring no hardships. Since I have lived in this pretty town I have become a worshiper of the goddess Gemutlichkeit. Perhaps I shan't find another home as dear to my heart as this has been, but at least I shan't have to sleep on a park bench, and any one can tell you that park benches have long been the favored resting place of genius. There is Frau Nirlanger beckoning us. Now do stop scowling, and smile for the lady. I know you will get on beautifully with the aborigines."

He did get on with them so beautifully that in less than half an hour they were swapping stories of Germany, of Austria, of the universities, of student life. Frau Knapf served a late supper, at which some one led in singing Auld Lang Syne, although the sounds emanating from the aborigines' end of the table sounded suspiciously like Die Wacht am Rhein. Following that the aborigines rose en masse and roared out their German university songs, banging their glasses on the table when they came to the chorus until we all caught the spirit of it and banged our glasses like rathskeller veterans. Then the red-faced and amorous Fritz, he of the absent Lena, announced his intention of entertaining the company. Made bold by an injudicious mixture of Herr Knapf's excellent beer, and a wonderful punch which Von Gerhard had concocted, Fritz mounted his chair, placed his plump hand over the spot where he supposed his heart to be, fastened his watery blue eyes upon my surprised and blushing countenance, and sang "Weh! Dass Wir Scheiden Mussen!" in an astonishingly beautiful barytone. I dared not look at Von Gerhard, for I knew that he was purple with suppressed mirth, so I stared stonily at the sardine sandwich and dill pickle on my plate, and felt myself growing hot and hysterical, and cold and tearful by turns.

At the end of the last verse I rose hastily and brought from their hiding-place the gifts which we of Knapfs' had purchased as remembrances for Herr and Frau Knapf. I had been delegated to make the presentation speech, so I grasped in one hand the too elaborate pipe that was to make Herr Knapf unhappy, and the too fashionable silk umbrella that was to appall Frau Knapf, and ascended the little platform at the end of the dining room, and began to speak in what I fondly thought to be fluent and highsounding German. Immediately the aborigines went off into paroxysms of laughter. They threw back their heads and roared, and slapped their thighs, and spluttered. It appeared that they thought I was making a humorous speech. At that discovery I cast dignity aside and continued my speech in the language of a German vaudeville comedian, with a dash of Weber and Field here and there. With the presentation of the silk umbrella Frau Knapf burst into tears, groped about helplessly for her apron, realized that it was missing from its accustomed place, and wiped her tears upon her cherished blue silk sleeve in the utter abandon of her sorrow. We drank to the future health and prosperity of our tearful host and hostess, and some one suggested drei mal drei, to which we responded in a manner to make the chin-chucking lieutenant tremble in his frame on the wall.

When it was all over Frau Nirlanger beckoned me, and she, Dr. von Gerhard and I stole out into the hall and stood at the foot of the stairway, discussing our plans for the future, and trying to smile as we talked of this plan and that. Frau Nirlanger, in the pretty white gown, was looking haggard and distrait. The oogly husband was still in the dining room, finishing the beer and punch, of which he had already taken too much.

"A tiny apartment we have taken," said Frau Nirlanger, softly. "It is better so. Then I shall have a little housework, a little cooking, a little marketing to keep me busy and perhaps happy." Her hand closed over mine. "But that shall us not separate," she pleaded. "Without you to make me sometimes laugh what should I then do? You will bring her often to our little apartment, not?" she went on, turning appealingly to Von Gerhard.

"As often as Mrs. Orme will allow me," he answered.

"Ach, yes. So lonely I shall be. You do not know what she has been to me, this Dawn. She is brave for two. Always laughing she is, and merry, nicht wahr? Meine kleine Soldatin, I call her."

"Soldatin, eh?" mused Von Gerhard. "Our little soldier. She is well named. And her battles she fights alone. But quite alone." His eyes, as they looked down on me from his great height had that in them which sent the blood rushing and tingling to my finger-tips. I brought my hand to my head in stiff military salute.

"Inspection satisfactory, sir?"

He laughed a rueful little laugh. "Eminently. Aber ganz befriedigend."

He was very tall, and straight and good to look at as he stood there in the hall with the light from the newel-post illuminating his features and emphasizing his blondness. Frau Nirlanger's face wore a drawn little look of pain as she gazed at him, and from him to the figure of her husband who had just emerged from the dining room, and was making unsteady progress toward us. Herr Nirlanger's face was flushed and his damp, dark hair was awry so that one lock straggled limply down over his forehead. As he approached he surveyed us with a surly frown that changed slowly into a leering grin. He lurched over and placed a hand familiarly on my shoulder.

"We mus' part," he announced, dramatically. "O, weh! The bes' of frien's m'z part. Well, g'by, li'l interfering Teufel. F'give you, though, b'cause you're such a pretty li'l Teufel." He raised one hand as though to pat my check and because of the horror which I saw on the face of the woman beside me I tried to smile, and did not shrink from him. But with a quick movement Von Gerhard clutched the swaying figure and turned it so that it faced the stairs.

"Come Nirlanger! Time for hard-working men like you and me to be in bed. Mrs. Orme must not nod over her desk to-morrow, either. So good-night. Schlafen Sie wohl."

Konrad Nirlanger turned a scowling face over his shoulder. Then he forgot what he was scowling for, and smiled a leering smile.

"Pretty good frien's, you an' the li'l Teufel, yes? Guess we'll have to watch you, huh, Anna? We'll watch 'em, won't we?"

He began to climb the stairs laboriously, with Frau Nirlanger's light figure flitting just ahead of him. At the bend in the stairway she turned and looked down on us a moment, her eyes very bright and big. She pressed her fingers to her lips and wafted a little kiss toward us with a gesture indescribably graceful and pathetic. She viewed her husband's laborious progress, not daring to offer help. Then the turn in the stair hid her from sight.

In the dim quiet of the little hallway Von Gerhard held out his hands—those deft, manual hands—those steady, sure, surgeonly hands—hands to cling to, to steady oneself by, and because I needed them most just then, and because I longed with my whole soul to place both my weary hands in those strong capable ones and to bring those dear, cool, sane fingers up to my burning cheeks, I put one foot on the first stair and held out two chilly fingertips. "Good-night, Herr Doktor," I said, "and thank you, not only for myself, but for her. I have felt what she feels to-night. It is not a pleasant thing to be ashamed of one's husband."

Von Gerhard's two hands closed over that one of mine. "Dawn, you will let me help you to find comfortable quarters? You cannot tramp about from place to place all the week. Let us get a list of addresses, and then, with the machine, we can drive from one to the other in an hour. It will at least save you time and strength."

"Go boarding-house hunting in a stunning green automobile!"

I exclaimed. From my vantage point on the steps I could look down on him, and there came over me a great longing to run my fingers gently through that crisp blond hair, and to bring his head down close against my breast for one exquisite moment. So—"Landladies and oitermobiles!" I laughed. "Never! Don't you know that if they got one glimpse, through the front parlor windows, of me stepping grand-like out of your green motor car, they would promptly over-charge me for any room in the house? I shall go room-hunting in my oldest hat, with one finger sticking out of my glove."

Von Gerhard shrugged despairing shoulders.

"Na, of what use is it to plead with you. Sometimes I wonder if, after all, you are not merely amusing yourself. Getting copy, perhaps, for the book, or a new experience to add to your already varied store."

Abruptly I turned to hide my pain, and began to ascend the stairs. With a bound Von Gerhard was beside me, his face drawn and contrite.

"Forgive me, Dawn! I know that you are wisest. It is only that I become a little mad, I think, when I see you battling alone like this, among strangers, and know that I have not the right to help you. I knew not what I was saying. Come, raise your eyes and smile, like the little Soldatin that you are. So. Now I am forgiven, yes?"

I smiled cheerily enough into his blue eyes. "Quite forgiven. And now you must run along. This is scandalously late. The aborigines will be along saying 'Morgen!' instead of 'Nabben'!' if we stay here much longer. Good-night."

"You will give me your new address as soon as you have found a satisfactory home?"

"Never fear! I probably shall be pestering you with telephone calls, urging you to have pity upon me in my loneliness. Now goodnight again. I'm as full of farewells as a Bernhardt." And to end it I ran up the stairs. At the bend, just where Frau Nirlanger had turned, I too stopped and looked over my shoulder. Von

Gerhard was standing as I had left him, looking up at me. And like Frau Nirlanger, I wafted a little kiss in his direction, before I allowed the bend in the stairs to cut off my view. But Von Gerhard did not signify by look or word that he had seen it, as he stood looking up at me, one strong white hand resting on the broad baluster.

CHAPTER XVI

JUNE MOONLIGHT, AND A NEW BOARDINGHOUSE

There was a week in which to scurry about for a new home. The days scampered by, tripping over one another in their haste. My sleeping hours were haunted by nightmares of landladies and impossible boarding-house bedrooms. Columns of "To Let, Furnished or Unfurnished" ads filed, advanced, and retreated before my dizzy eyes. My time after office hours was spent in climbing dim stairways, interviewing unenthusiastic females in kimonos, and peering into ugly bedrooms papered with sprawly and impossible patterns and filled with the odors of dead-and-gone dinners. I found one room less impossible than the rest, only to be told that the preference was to be given to a man who had "looked" the day before.

"I d'ruther take gents only," explained the ample person who carried the keys to the mansion. "Gents goes early in the morning and comes in late at night, and that's all you ever see of 'em, half the time. I've tried ladies, an' they get me wild, always yellin' for hot water to wash their hair, or pastin' handkerchiefs up on the mirr'r or wantin' to butt into the kitchen to press this or that. I'll let you know if the gent don't take it, but I got an idea he will."

He did. At any rate, no voice summoned me to that haven for gents only. There were other landladies—landladies fat and German; landladies lean and Irish; landladies loquacious (regardless of nationality); landladies reserved; landladies husbandless, wedded, widowed, divorced, and willing;

landladies slatternly; landladies prim; and all hinting of past estates wherein there had been much grandeur.

At last, when despair gripped me, and I had horrid visions of my trunk, hat-box and typewriter reposing on the sidewalk while I, homeless, sat perched in the midst of them, I chanced upon a room which commanded a glorious view of the lake. True, it was too expensive for my slim purse; true, the owner of it was sour of feature; true, the room itself was cavernous and unfriendly and cold-looking, but the view of the great, blue lake triumphed over all these, although a cautious inner voice warned me that that lake view would cover a multitude of sins. I remembered, later, how she of the sour visage had dilated upon the subject of the sunrise over the water. I told her at the time that while I was passionately fond of sunrises myself, still I should like them just as well did they not occur so early in the morning. Whereupon she of the vinegar countenance had sniffed. I loathe landladies who sniff.

My trunk and trusty typewriter were sent on to my new home at noon, unchaperoned, for I had no time to spare at that hour of the day. Later I followed them, laden with umbrella, boxes, brown-paper parcels, and other unfashionable moving-day paraphernalia. I bumped and banged my way up the two flights of stairs that led to my lake view and my bed, and my heart went down as my feet went up. By the time the cavernous bedroom was gained I felt decidedly quivery-mouthed, so that I dumped my belongings on the floor in a heap and went to the window to gaze on the lake until my spirits should rise. But it was a gray day, and the lake looked large, and wet and unsociable. You couldn't get chummy with it. I turned to my great barn of a room. You couldn't get chummy with that, either. I began to unpack, with furious energy. In vain I turned every gas jet blazing high. They only cast dim shadows in the murky vastness of that awful chamber. A whole Fourth of July fireworks display, Roman candles, sky-rockets, pin-wheels, set pieces and all, could not have made that room take on a festive air.

As I unpacked I thought of my cosy room at Knapfs', and as I thought I took my head out of my trunk and sank down on the floor with a satin blouse in one hand, and a walking boot in the other, and wanted to bellow with loneliness. There came to me dear visions of the friendly old yellow brocade chair, and the lamplight, and the fireplace, and Frau Nirlanger, and the Pfannkuchen. I thought of the aborigines. In my homesick mind their bumpy faces became things of transcendent beauty. I could have put my head on their combined shoulders and wept down their blue satin neckties. In my memory of Frau Knapf it seemed to me that I could discern a dim, misty halo hovering above her tightly wadded hair. My soul went out to her as I recalled the shining cheek-bones, and the apron, and the chickens stewed in butter. I would have given a year out of my life to have heard that good-natured, "Nabben!" One aborigine had been wont to emphasize his after-dinner arguments with a toothpick brandished fiercely between thumb and finger. The brandisher had always annoyed me. Now I thought of him with tenderness in my heart and reproached myself for my fastidiousness. I should have wept if I had not had a walking boot in one hand, and a satin blouse in the other. A walking boot is but a cold comfort. And my thriftiness denied my tears the soiling of the blouse. So I sat up on my knees and finished the unpacking.

Just before dinner time I donned a becoming gown to chirk up my courage, groped my way down the long, dim stairs, and telephoned to Von Gerhard. It seemed to me that just to hear his voice would instill in me new courage and hope. I gave the number, and waited.

"Dr. von Gerhard?" repeated a woman's voice at the other end of the wire. "He is very busy. Will you leave your name?"

"No," I snapped. "I'll hold the wire. Tell him that Mrs. Orme is waiting to speak to him."

"I'll see." The voice was grudging.

Another wait; then—"Dawn!" came his voice in glad surprise.

"Hello!" I cried, hysterically. "Hello! Oh, talk! Say something nice, for pity's sake! I'm sorry that I've taken you away from whatever you were doing, but I couldn't help it. Just talk please! I'm dying of loneliness."

"Child, are you ill?" Von Gerhard's voice was so satisfyingly solicitous. "Is anything wrong? Your voice is trembling. I can hear it quite plainly. What has happened? Has Norah written—"

"Norah? No. There was nothing in her letter to upset me. It is only the strangeness of this place. I shall be all right in a day or so."

"The new home—it is satisfactory? You have found what you wanted? Your room is comfortable?"

"It's—it's a large room," I faltered. "And there's a—a large view of the lake, too."

There was a smothered sound at the other end of the wire. Then—"I want you to meet me down-town at seven o'clock. We will have dinner together," Von Gerhard said, "I cannot have you moping up there all alone all evening."

"I can't come."

"Why?"

"Because I want to so very much. And anyway, I'm much more cheerful now. I am going in to dinner. And after dinner I shall get acquainted with my room. There are six corners and all the space under the bed that I haven't explored yet."

"Dawn!"

"Yes?"

"If you were free to-night, would you marry me? If you knew that the next month would find you mistress of yourself would you—"

"Ernst!"

"Yes?"

"If the gates of Heaven were opened wide to you, and they had 'Welcome!' done in diamonds over the door, and all the loveliest angel ladies grouped about the doorway to receive you, and just beyond you could see awaiting you all that was beautiful, and most exquisite, and most desirable, would you enter?"

And then I hung up the receiver and went in to dinner. I went in to dinner, but not to dine. Oh, shades of those who have suffered in boarding-houses—that dining room! It must have been patterned after the dining room at Dotheboys' hall. It was bare, and cheerless, and fearfully undressed looking. The diners were seated at two long, unsociable, boarding-housey tables that ran the length of the room, and all the women folks came down to dine with white wool shawls wrapped snugly about their susceptible black silk shoulders. The general effect was that of an Old People's Home. I found seat after seat at table was filled, and myself the youngest thing present. I felt so criminally young that I wondered they did not strap me in a high chair and ram bread and milk down my throat. Now and then the door would open to admit another snuffly, ancient, and be-shawled member of the company. I learned that Mrs. Schwartz, on my right, did not care mooch for shteak for breakfast, aber a leedle l'mb ch'p she likes. Also that the elderly party on my left and the elderly party on my right resented being separated by my person. Conversation between E. P. on right, and E. P. on left scintillated across my soup, thus:

"How you feel this evening Mis' Maurer, h'm?"

"Don't ask me."

"No wonder you got rheumatism. My room was like a ice-house all day. Yours too?"

"I don't complain any more. Much good it does. Barley soup again? In my own home I never ate it, and here I pay my good money and get four time a week barley soup. Are those fresh cucumbers? M-m-m-m. They haven't stood long enough. Look at Mis' Miller. She feels good this evening. She should feel good. Twenty-five cents she won at bridge. I never seen how that woman is got luck."

I choked, gasped, and fled.

Back in my own mausoleum once more I put things in order, dragged my typewriter stand into the least murky corner under the bravest gas jet and rescued my tottering reason by turning out a long letter to Norah. That finished, my spirits rose. I dived into the bottom of my trunk for the loose sheets of the book-in-the-making, glanced over the last three or four, discovered that they did not sound so maudlin as I had feared, and straightway forgot my gloomy surroundings in the fascination of weaving the tale.

In the midst of my fine frenzy there came a knock at the door. In the hall stood the anemic little serving maid who had attended me at dinner. She was almost eclipsed by a huge green pasteboard box.

"You're Mis' Orme, ain't you? This here's for you."

The little white-cheeked maid hovered at the threshold while I lifted the box cover and revealed the perfection of the American beauty buds that lay there, all dewy and fragrant. The eyes of the little maid were wide with wonder as she gazed, and because I had known flower-hunger I separated two stately blossoms from the glowing cluster and held them out to her.

"For me!" she gasped, and brought her lips down to them, gently. Then—"There's a high green jar downstairs you can have to stick your flowers in. You ain't got nothin' big enough in here, except your water pitcher. An' putting these grand flowers in a water pitcher—why, it'd be like wearing a silk dress over a flannel petticoat, wouldn't it?"

When the anemic little boarding-house slavey with the beauty-loving soul had fetched the green jar, I placed the shining stems in it with gentle fingers. At the bottom of the box I found a card that read: "For it is impossible to live in a room with red roses and still be traurig."

How well he knew! And how truly impossible to be sad when red roses are glowing for one, and filling the air with their fragrance!

The interruption was fatal to book-writing. My thoughts were a chaos of red roses, and anemic little maids with glowing eyes, and thoughtful young doctors with a marvelous understanding of feminine moods. So I turned out all the lights, undressed by moonlight, and, throwing a kimono about me, carried my jar of roses to the window and sat down beside them so that their exquisite scent caressed me.

The moonlight had put a spell of white magic upon the lake. It was a light-flooded world that lay below my window. Summer, finger on lip, had stolen in upon the heels of spring. Dim, shadowy figures dotted the benches of the park across the way. Just beyond lay the silver lake, a dazzling bar of moonlight on its breast. Motors rushed along the roadway with a roar and a whir and were gone, leaving a trail of laughter behind them. From the open window of the room below came the slip-slap of cards on the polished table surface, and the low buzz of occasional conversation as the players held postmortems. Under the street light the popcorn vender's cart made a blot on the mystic beauty of the scene below. But the perfume of my red roses came to me, and their velvet caressed my check, and beyond the noise and lights of the street lay that glorious lake with the bar of moonlight on its soft breast. I gazed and forgave the sour-faced landlady her dining room; forgave the elderly parties their shawls and barley soup; forgot for a moment my weary thoughts of Peter Orme; forgot everything except that it was June, and moonlight and good to be alive.

All the changes and events of that strange, eventful year came crowding to my mind as I crouched there at the window. Four new friends, tried and true! I conned them over joyously in my heart. What a strange contrast they made! Blackie, of the elastic morals, and the still more elastic heart; Frau Nirlanger, of the smiling lips and the lilting voice and the tragic eyes— she who had stooped from a great height to pluck the flower of love blooming below, only to find a worthless weed sullying her hand; Alma Pflugel, with the unquenchable light of gratefulness in her honest face; Von Gerhard, ready to act as buffer between myself and the world, tender as a woman, gravely thoughtful, with the light of devotion glowing in his steady eyes.

"Here's richness," said I, like the fat boy in Pickwick Papers.

And I thanked God for the new energy which had sent me to this lovely city by the lake. I thanked Him that I had not been content to remain a burden to Max and Norah, growing sour and crabbed with the years. Those years of work and buffeting had made of me a broader, finer, truer type of womanhood—had caused me to forget my own little tragedy in contemplating the great human comedy. And so I made a little prayer there in the moon-flooded room.

"O dear Lord," I prayed, and I did not mean that it should sound irreverent. "O dear Lord, don't bother about my ambitions! Just let me remain strong and well enough to do the work that is my portion from day to day. Keep me faithful to my standards of right and wrong. Let this new and wonderful love which has come into my life be a staff of strength and comfort instead of a burden of weariness. Let me not grow careless and slangy as the years go by. Let me keep my hair and complexion and teeth, and deliver me from wearing soiled blouses and doing my hair in a knob. Amen."

I felt quite cheerful after that—so cheerful that the strange bumps in the new bed did not bother me as unfamiliar beds usually did. The roses I put to sleep in their jar of green, keeping one to hold against my cheek as I slipped into dreamland. I thought drowsily, just before sleep claimed me:

"To-morrow, after office hours, I'll tuck up my skirt, and wrap my head in a towel and have a housecleaning bee. I'll move the bed where the wash-stand is now, and I'll make the chiffonnier swap places with the couch. One feels on friendlier terms with furniture that one has shoved about a little. How brilliant the moonlight is! The room is flooded with it. Those roses—sweet!—sweet!—"

When I awoke it was morning. During the days that followed I looked back gratefully upon that night, with its moonlight, and its roses, and its great peace.

CHAPTER XVII

THE SHADOW OF TERROR

Two days before the date set for Von Gerhard's departure the book was finished, typed, re-read, packed, and sent away. Half an hour after it was gone all its most glaring faults seemed to marshall themselves before my mind's eye. Whole paragraphs, that had read quite reasonably before, now loomed ludicrous in perspective. I longed to snatch it back; to tidy it here, to take it in there, to smooth certain rough places neglected in my haste. For almost a year I had lived with this thing, so close that its faults and its virtues had become indistinguishable to me. Day and night, for many months, it had been in my mind. Of late some instinct had prompted me to finish it. I had worked at it far into the night, until I marveled that the ancient occupants of the surrounding rooms did not enter a combined protest against the clack-clacking of my typewriter keys. And now that it was gone I wondered, dully, if I could feel Von Gerhard's departure more keenly.

No one knew of the existence of the book except Norah, Von Gerhard, Blackie and me. Blackie had a way of inquiring after its progress in hushed tones of mock awe. Also he delighted in getting down on hands and knees and guiding a yard-stick carefully about my desk with a view to having a fence built around it, bearing an inscription which would inform admiring tourists that here was the desk at which the brilliant author had been wont to sit when grinding out heart-throb stories for the humble Post. He took an impish delight in my struggles with my hero and heroine, and his inquiries after the health of both were of such a nature as to make any earnest writer person rise in wrath and slay him. I had seen little of Blackie of late. My spare hours had been devoted to the work in hand. On the day after the book was sent away I was conscious of a little shock as I strolled into Blackie's sanctum and took my accustomed seat beside his big desk. There was an oddly pinched look about Blackie's nostrils and lips, I thought. And the deep-set black eyes appeared deeper and blacker than ever in his thin little face.

A week of unseasonable weather had come upon the city. June was going out in a wave of torrid heat such as August might have boasted. The day had seemed endless and intolerably close. I was feeling very limp and languid. Perhaps, thought I, it was the heat which had wilted Blackie's debonair spirits.

"It has been a long time since we've had a talk-talk, Blackie. I've missed you. Also you look just a wee bit green around the edges. I'm thinking a vacation wouldn't hurt you."

Blackie's lean brown forefinger caressed the bowl of his favorite pipe. His eyes, that had been gazing out across the roofs beyond his window, came back to me, and there was in them a curious and quizzical expression as of one who is inwardly amused.

"I've been thinkin' about a vacation. None of your measly little two weeks' affairs, with one week on salary, and th' other without. I ain't goin' t' take my vacation for a while—not till fall, p'raps, or maybe winter. But w'en I do take it, sa-a-ay, girl, it's goin' t' be a real one."

"But why wait so long?" I asked. "You need it now. Who ever heard of putting off a vacation until winter!"

"Well, I dunno," mused Blackie. "I just made my arrangements for that time, and I hate t' muss 'em up. You'll say, w'en the time comes, that my plans are reasonable."

There was a sharp ring from the telephone at Blackie's elbow. He answered it, then thrust the receiver into my hand. "For you," he said.

It was Von Gerhard's voice that came to me. "I have

something to tell you," he said. "Something most important. If I call for you at six we can drive out to the bay for supper, yes? I must talk to you."

"You have saved my life," I called back. "It has been a beast of a day. You may talk as much and as importantly as you like, so long as I am kept cool."

"That was Von Gerhard," said I to Blackie, and tried not to look uncomfortable.

"Mm," grunted Blackie, pulling at his pipe. "Thoughtful, ain't he?"

I turned at the door. "He—he's going away day after to-morrow, Blackie," I explained, although no explanation had been asked for, "to Vienna. He expects to stay a year—or two—or three—"

Blackie looked up quickly. "Goin' away, is he? Well, maybe it's best, all around, girl. I see his name's been mentioned in all the medical papers, and the big magazines, and all that, lately. Gettin' t' be a big bug, Von Gerhard is. Sorry he's goin', though. I was plannin' t' consult him just before I go on my—vacation. But some other guy'll do. He don't approve of me, Von Gerhard don't."

For some reason which I could never explain I went back into the room and held out both my hands to Blackie. His nervous brown fingers closed over them. "That doesn't make one bit of difference to us, does it, Blackie?" I said, gravely. "We're—we're not caring so long as we approve of one another, are we?"

"Not a bit, girl," smiled Blackie, "not a bit."

When the green car stopped before the Old Folks' Home I was in seraphic mood. I had bathed, donned clean linen and a Dutch-necked gown. The result was most soul-satisfying. My spirits rose unaccountably. Even the sight of Von Gerhard, looking troubled and distrait, did not quiet them. We darted away, out along the lake front, past the toll gate, to the bay road stretching its flawless length along the water's side. It was alive with swift-moving motor cars swarming like twentieth-century pilgrims toward the mecca of cool breezes and comfort. There were proud limousines; comfortable family cars; trim little roadsters; noisy runabouts. Not a hoof-beat was to be heard. It was as though the horseless age had indeed descended upon the world. There was only a hum, a rush, a roar, as car after car swept on.

Summer homes nestled among the trees near the lake. Through the branches one caught occasional gleams of silvery water. The rush of cool air fanned my hot forehead, tousled my hair, slid down between my collar and the back of my neck, and I was grandly content.

"Even though you are going to sail away, and even though you have the grumps, and refuse to talk, and scowl like a jabberwock, this is an extremely nice world. You can't spoil it."

"Behute!" Von Gerhard's tone was solemn.

"Would you be faintly interested in knowing that the book is finished?"

"So? That is well. You were wearing yourself thin over it. It was then quickly perfected."

"Perfected!" I groaned. "I turn cold when I think of it. The last chapters got away from me completely. They lacked the punch."

Von Gerhard considered that a moment, as I wickedly had intended that he should. Then—"The punch? What is that then—the punch?"

Obligingly I elucidated. "A book may be written in flawless style, with a plot, and a climax, and a lot of little side surprises. But if it lacks that peculiar and convincing quality poetically known as the punch, it might as well never have been written. It can never be a six-best-seller, neither will it live as a classic. You will never see it advertised on the book review page of the Saturday papers, nor will the man across the aisle in the street car be so absorbed in its contents that he will be taken past his corner."

Von Gerhard looked troubled. "But the literary value? Does that not enter—"

"I don't aim to contribute to the literary uplift," I assured him. "All my life I have cherished two ambitions. One of them is to write a successful book, and the other to learn to whistle through my teeth—this way, you know, as the gallery gods do it. I am almost despairing of the whistle, but I still have hopes of the book."

Whereupon Von Gerhard, after a moment's stiff surprise, gave vent to one of his heartwarming roars.

"Thanks," said I. "Now tell me the important news."

His face grew serious in an instant. "Not yet, Dawn. Later. Let us hear more about the book. Not so flippant, however, small one. The time is past when you can deceive me with your nonsense."

"Surely you would not have me take myself seriously! That's another debt I owe my Irish forefathers. They could laugh—bless 'em!—in the very teeth of a potato crop failure. And let me tell you, that takes some sense of humor. The book is my potato crop. If it fails it will mean that I must keep on drudging, with a knot or two taken in my belt. But I'll squeeze a smile out of the corner of my mouth, somehow. And if it succeeds! Oh, Ernst, if it succeeds!"

"Then, Kindchen?"

"Then it means that I may have a little thin layer of jam on my bread and butter. It won't mean money—at least, I don't think it will. A first book never does. But it will mean a future. It will mean that I will have something solid to stand on. It will be a real beginning—a breathing spell—time in which to accomplish something really worth while—independence—freedom from this tread-mill—"

"Stop!" cried Von Gerhard, sharply. Then, as I stared in surprise—"I do ask your pardon. I was again rude, nicht wahr? But in me there is a queer vein of German superstition that disapproves of air castles. Sich einbilden, we call it."

The lights of the bay pavilion twinkled just ahead. The green car poked its nose up the path between rows of empty machines.

At last it drew up, panting, before a vacant space between an imposing, scarlet touring car and a smart, cream-colored runabout. We left it there and walked up the light-flooded path.

Inside the great, barn-like structure that did duty as pavilion glasses clinked, chairs scraped on the wooden floor; a burst of music followed a sharp fusillade of applause. Through the open doorway could be seen a company of Tyrolese singers in picturesque costumes of scarlet and green and black. The scene was very noisy, and very bright, and very German.

"Not in there, eh?" said Von Gerhard, as though divining my wish. "It is too brightly lighted, and too noisy. We will find a table out here under the trees, where the music is softened by the distance, and our eyes are not offended by the ugliness of the singers. But inexcusably ugly they are, these Tyrolese women."

We found a table within the glow of the pavilion's lights, but still so near the lake that we could hear the water lapping the shore. A cadaverous, sandy-haired waiter brought things to eat, and we made brave efforts to appear hungry and hearty, but my high spirits were ebbing fast, and Von Gerhard was frankly distraught. One of the women singers appeared suddenly in the doorway of the pavilion, then stole down the steps, and disappeared in the shadow of the trees beyond our table. The voices of the singers ceased abruptly. There was a moment's hushed silence. Then, from the shadow of the trees came a woman's voice, clear, strong, flexible, flooding the night with the bird-like trill of the mountain yodel. The sound rose and fell, and swelled and soared. A silence. Then, in a great burst of melody the chorus of voices within the pavilion answered the call. Again a silence. Again the wonder of the woman's voice flooded the stillness, ending in a note higher, clearer, sweeter than any that had gone before. Then the little Tyrolese, her moment of glory ended, sped into the light of the noisy pavilion again.

When I turned to Von Gerhard my eyes were wet. "I shall have that to remember, when you are gone."

Von Gerhard beckoned the hovering waiter. "Take these

things away. And you need not return." He placed something in the man's palm—something that caused a sudden whisking away of empty dishes, and many obsequious bows.

Von Gerhard's face was turned away from me, toward the beauty of the lake and sky. Now, as the last flirt of the waiter's apron vanished around the corner he turned his head slowly, and I saw that in his eyes which made me catch my breath with apprehension.

"What is it?" I cried. "Norah? Max? The children?"

He shook his head. "They are well, so far, as I know. I—perhaps first I should tell you—although this is not the thing which I have to say to you—"

"Yes?" I urged him on, impatiently. I had never seen him like this.

"I do not sail this week. I shall not be with Gluck in Vienna this year. I shall stay here."

"Here! Why? Surely—"

"Because I shall be needed here, Dawn. Because I cannot leave you now. You will need—some one—a friend—"

I stared at him with eyes that were wide with terror, waiting for I knew not what.

"Need—some one—for—what?" I stammered. "Why should you—"

In the kindly shadow of the trees Von Gerhard's hands took my icy ones, and held them in a close clasp of encouragement.

"Norah is coming to be with you—"

"Norah! Why? Tell me at once! At once!"

"Because Peter Orme has been sent home—cured," said he.

The lights of the pavilion fell away, and advanced, and swung about in a great sickening circle. I shut my eyes. The lights still swung before my eyes. Von Gerhard leaned toward me with a word of alarm. I clung to his hands with all my strength.

"No!" I said, and the savage voice was not my own. "No! No! No! It isn't true! It isn't—Oh, it's some joke, isn't it? Tell me, it's—it's something funny, isn't it? And after a bit we'll laugh—we'll laugh—of course—see! I am smiling already—"

"Dawn—dear one—it is true. God knows I wish that I could be happy to know it. The hospital authorities pronounce him cured. He has been quite sane for weeks."

"You knew it—how long?"

"You know that Max has attended to all communications from the doctors there. A few weeks ago they wrote that Orme had shown evidences of recovery. He spoke of you, of the people he had known in New York, of his work on the paper, all quite rationally and calmly. But they must first be sure. Max went to New York a week ago. Peter was gone. The hospital authorities were frightened and apologetic. Peter had walked away quite coolly one day. He had gone into the city, borrowed money of some old newspaper cronies, and vanished. He may be there still. He may be—"

"Here! Ernst! Take me home! O God; I can't do it! I can't! I ought to be happy, but I'm not. I ought to be thankful, but I'm not, I'm not! The horror of having him there was great enough, but it was nothing compared to the horror of having him here. I used to dream that he was well again, and that he was searching for me, and the dreadful realness of it used to waken me, and I would find myself shivering with terror. Once I dreamed that I looked up from my desk to find him standing in the doorway, smiling that mirthless smile of his, and I heard him say, in his mocking way: 'Hello, Dawn my love; looking wonderfully well. Grass widowhood agrees with you, eh?'"

"Dawn, you must not laugh like that. Come, we will go. You are shivering! Don't, dear, don't. See, you have Norah, and Max, and me to help you. We will put him on his feet. Physically he is not what he should be. I can do much for him."

"You!" I cried, and the humor of it was too exquisite for laughter.

"For that I gave up Vienna," said Von Gerhard, simply. "You, too, must do your share."

"My share! I have done my share. He was in the gutter, and

he was dragging me with him. When his insanity came upon him I thanked God for it, and struggled up again. Even Norah never knew what that struggle was. Whatever I am, I am in spite of him. I tell you I could hug my widow's weeds. Ten years ago he showed me how horrible and unclean a thing can be made of this beautiful life. I was a despairing, cowering girl of twenty then—I am a woman now, happy in her work, her friends; growing broader and saner in thought, quicker to appreciate the finer things in life. And now—what?"

They were dashing off a rollicking folk-song indoors. When it was finished there came a burst of laughter and the sharp spat of applauding hands, and shouts of approbation. The sounds seemed seared upon my brain. I rose and ran down the path toward the waiting machine. There in the darkness I buried my shamed face in my hands and prayed for the tears that would not come.

It seemed hours before I heard Von Gerhard's firm, quick tread upon the gravel path. He moved about the machine, adjusting this and that, then took his place at the wheel without a word. We glided out upon the smooth white road. All the loveliness of the night seemed to have vanished. Only the ugly, distorted shadows remained. The terror of uncertainty gripped me. I could not endure the sight of Von Gerhard's stern, set face. I grasped his arm suddenly so that the machine veered and darted across the road. With a mighty wrench Von Gerhard righted it. He stopped the machine at the road-side.

"Careful, Kindchen," he said, gravely.

"Ernst," I said, and my breath came quickly, chokingly, as though I had been running fast, "Ernst, I can't do it. I'm not big enough. I can't. I hate him, I tell you, I hate him! My life is my own. I've made it what it is, in the face of a hundred temptations; in spite of a hundred pitfalls. I can't lay it down again for Peter Orme to trample. Ernst, if you love me, take me away now. To Vienna—anywhere—only don't ask me to take up my life with him again. I can't—I can't—"

"Love you?" repeated Ernst, slowly, "yes. Too well—"

"Too well—"

"Yes, too well for that, Gott sei dank, small one. Too well for that."

CHAPTER XVIII

PETER ORME

A man's figure rose from the shadows of the porch and came forward to meet us as we swung up to the curbing. I stifled a scream in my throat. As I shrank back into the seat I heard the quick intake of Von Gerhard's breath as he leaned forward to peer into the darkness. A sick dread came upon me.

"Sa-a-ay, girl," drawled the man's voice, with a familiar little cackling laugh in it, "sa-a-ay, girl, the policeman on th' beat's got me spotted for a suspicious character. I been hoofin' it up an' down this block like a distracted mamma waitin' for her daughter t' come home from a boat ride."

"Blackie! It's only you!"

"Thanks, flatterer," simpered Blackie, coming to the edge of the walk as I stepped from the automobile. "Was you expectin' the landlady?"

"I don't know just whom I expected. I—I'm nervous, I think, and you startled me. Dr. Von Gerhard was taken back for a moment, weren't you, Doctor?"

Von Gerhard laughed ruefully. "Frankly, yes. It is not early. And visitors at this hour—"

"What in the world is it, Blackie?" I put in. "Don't tell me that Norberg has been seized with one of his fiendish inspirations at this time of night."

Blackie struck a match and held it for an instant so that the flare of it illuminated his face as he lighted his cigarette. There was no laughter in the deep-set black eyes.

"What is it Blackie?" I asked again. The horror of what Von

Gerhard had told me made the prospect of any lesser trial a welcome relief.

"I got t' talk to you for a minute. P'raps Von Gerhard 'd better hear it, too. I telephoned you an hour ago. Tried to get you out to the bay. Waited here ever since. Got a parlor, or somethin', where a guy can talk?"

I led the way indoors. The first floor seemed deserted. The bare, unfriendly boarding-house parlor was unoccupied, and one dim gas jet did duty as illumination.

"Bring in the set pieces," muttered Blackie, as he turned two more gas jets flaring high. "This parlor just yells for a funeral."

Von Gerhard was frowning. "Mrs. Orme is not well," he began. "She has had a shock—some startling news concerning—"

"Her husband?" inquired Blackie, coolly. I started up with a cry. "How could you know?"

A look of relief came into Blackie's face. "That helps a little. Now listen, kid. An' w'en I get through, remember I'm there with the little helpin' mitt. Have a cigarette, Doc?"

"No," said Von Gerhard, shortly.

Blackie's strange black eyes were fastened on my face, and I saw an expression of pity in their depths as he began to talk.

"I was up at the Press Club to-night. Dropped in for a minute or two, like I always do on the rounds. The place sounded kind of still when I come up the steps, and I wondered where all the boys was. Looked into the billiard room—nothin' doin'. Poked my head in at the writin' room—same. Ambled into the readin' room—empty. Well, I steered for the dining room, an' there was the bunch. An' just as I come in they give a roar, and I started to investigate. Up against the fireplace, with one hand in his pocket, and the other hanging careless like on the mantel, stood a man—stranger t' me. He was talkin' kind of low, and quick, bitin' off his words like a Englishman. An' the boys, they was starin' with their eyes, an' their mouths, and forgettin' t' smoke, an' lettin' their pipes an' cigars go dead in their hands, while he talked. Talk! Sa-a-ay, girl, that guy, he could talk the leads right out of a ruled, locked form. I didn't catch his name. Tall, thin, unearthly lookin' chap, with the whitest teeth you ever saw, an' eyes—well, his eyes was somethin' like a lighted pipe with a little fine ash over the red, just waitin' for a sudden pull t' make it glow."

"Peter!" I moaned, and buried my face in my hands. Von Gerhard put a quick hand on my arm. But I shook it off. "I'm not going to faint," I said, through set teeth. "I'm not going to do anything silly. I want to think. I want to... Go on, Blackie."

"Just a minute," interrupted Von Gerhard. "Does he know where Mrs. Orme is living?"

"I'm coming t' that," returned Blackie, tranquilly. "Though for Dawn's sake I'll say right here he don't know. I told him later, that she was takin' a vacation up at her folks' in Michigan."

"Thank God!" I breathed.

"Wore a New York Press Club button, this guy did. I asked one of the boys standin' on the outer edge of the circle what the fellow's name was, but he only says: 'Shut up Black! An' listen. He's seen every darn thing in the world.' Well, I listened. He wasn't braggin'. He wasn't talkin' big. He was just talkin'. Seems like he'd been war correspondent in the Boer war, and the Spanish-American, an' Gawd knows where. He spoke low, not usin' any big words, either, an' I thought his eyes looked somethin' like those of the Black Cat up on the mantel just over his head—you know what I mean, when the electric lights is turned on in-inside{sic} the ugly thing. Well, every time he showed signs of stoppin', one of the boys would up with a question, and start him goin' again. He knew everybody, an' everything, an' everywhere. All of a sudden one of the boys points to the Roosevelt signature on the wall—the one he scrawled up there along with all the other celebrities first time he was entertained by the Press Club boys. Well this guy, he looked at the name for a minute. 'Roosevelt?' he says, slow. 'Oh, yes. Seems t' me I've heard of him.' Well, at that the boys yelled. Thought it was a good joke, seein' that Ted had been smeared all over the first page of everything for years. But kid, I seen th' look in that man's eyes when he said it, and he wasn't jokin', girl. An' it came t' me, all of a sudden, that all the things he'd been talkin' about had happened almost ten years back. After he'd made that break about Roosevelt he kind of shut up, and strolled over to the piano and began t' play. You know that bum old piano, with half a dozen dead keys, and no tune?"

I looked up for a moment. "He could make you think that it was a concert grand, couldn't he? He hasn't forgotten even that?"

"Forgotten? Girl, I don't know what his accomplishments was when you knew him, but if he was any more fascinatin' than he is now, then I'm glad I didn't know him. He could charm the pay envelope away from a reporter that was Saturday broke. Somethin' seemed t' urge me t' go up t' him an' say: 'Have a game of billiards?'

"'Don't care if I do,' says he, and swung his long legs off the piano stool and we made for the billiard room, with the whole gang after us. Sa-a-ay, girl, I'm a modest violet, I am, but I don't mind mentionin' that the general opinion up at the club is that I'm a little wizard with the cue. Well, w'en he got through with me I looked like little sister when big brother is tryin' t' teach her how to hold the cue in her fingers. He just sent them balls wherever he thought they'd look pretty. I bet if he'd held up his thumb and finger an' said, 'jump through this!' them balls would of jumped."

Von Gerhard took a couple of quick steps in Blackie's direction. His eyes were blue steel.

"Is this then necessary?" he asked. "All this leads to what? Has not Mrs. Orme suffered enough, that she should undergo this idle chatter? It is sufficient that she knows this—this man is here. It is a time for action, not for words."

"Action's comin' later, Doc," drawled Blackie, looking impish. "Monologuin' ain't my specialty. I gener'ly let the other gink talk. You never can learn nothin' by talkin'. But I got somethin' t' say t' Dawn here. Now, in case you're bored the least bit, w'y don't hesitate one minnit t'—"

"Na, you are quite right, and I was hasty," said Von Gerhard, and his eyes, with the kindly gleam in them, smiled down upon the little man. "It is only that both you and I are over-anxious to be of assistance to this unhappy lady. Well, we shall see. You talked with this man at the Press Club?"

"He talked. I listened."

"That would be Peter's way," I said, bitterly. "How he used to love to hold forth, and how I grew to long for blessed silence—for fewer words, and more of that reserve which means strength!"

"All this time," continued Blackie, "I didn't know his name. When we'd finished our game of billiards he hung up his cue, and then he turned around like lightning, and faced the boys that were standing around with their hands in their pockets. He had a odd little smile on his face—a smile with no fun it, if you know what I mean. Guess you do, maybe, if you've seen it.

"'Boys,' says he, smilin' that twisted kind of smile, 'boys, I'm lookin' for a job. I'm not much of a talker, an' I'm only a amateur at music, and my game of billiards is ragged. But there's one thing I can do, fellows, from abc up to xyz, and that's write. I can write, boys, in a way to make your pet little political scribe sound like a high school paper. I don't promise to stick. As soon as I get on my feet again I'm going back to New York. But not just yet. Meanwhile, I'm going to the highest bidder.'

"Well, you know since Merkle left us we haven't had a day when we wasn't scooped on some political guff. 'I guess we can use you—some place,' I says, tryin' not t' look too anxious. If your ideas on salary can take a slump be tween New York and Milwaukee. Our salaries around here is more what is elegantly known as a stipend. What's your name, Bo?'

"'Name?' says he, smiling again, 'Maybe it'll be familiar t' you. That is, it will if my wife is usin' it. Orme's my name—Peter Orme. Know a lady of that name? Good.'

"I hadn't said I did, but those eyes of his had seen the look on my face.

"'Friends in New York told me she was here,' he says. 'Where is she now? Got her address?' he says.

"'She expectin' you?' I asked.

"'N-not exactly,' he says, with that crooked grin.

"'Thought not,' I answered, before I knew what I was sayin'. 'She's up north with her folks on a vacation.'

"'The devil she is!' he says. 'Well, in that case can you let me have ten until Monday?'"

Blackie came over to me as I sat cowering in my chair. He patted my shoulder with one lean brown hand. "Now kid, you dig, see? Beat it. Go home for a week. I'll fix it up with Norberg. No tellin' what a guy like that's goin' t' do. Send your brother-in-law down here if you want to make it a family affair, and between us, we'll see this thing through."

I looked up at Von Gerhard. He was nodding approval. It all seemed so easy, so temptingly easy. To run away! Not to face him until I was safe in the shelter of Norah's arms! I stood up, resolve lending me new strength and courage.

"I am going. I know it isn't brave, but I can't be brave any longer. I'm too tired—too old—"

I grasped the hand of each of those men who had stood by me so staunchly in the year that was past. The words of thanks that I had on my lips ended in dry, helpless sobs. And because Blackie and Von Gerhard looked so pathetically concerned and so unhappy in my unhappiness my sobs changed to hysterical laughter, in which the two men joined, after one moment's bewildered staring.

So it was that we did not hear the front door slam, or the sound of footsteps in the hall. Our overstrained nerves found relief in laughter, so that Peter Orme, a lean, ominous figure in the doorway looked in upon a merry scene.

I was the first to see him. And at the sight of the emaciated figure, with its hollow cheeks and its sunken eyes all terror and hatred left me, and I felt only a great pity for this wreck of manhood. Slowly I went up to him there in the doorway.

"Well, Peter?" I said.

"Well, Dawn old girl," said he "you're looking wonderfully fit. Grass widowhood seems to agree with you, eh?"

And I knew then that my dread dream had come true.

Peter advanced into the room with his old easy grace of manner. His eyes glowed as he looked at Blackie. Then he laughed, showing his even, white teeth. "Why, you little liar!" he said, in his crisp, clear English. "I've a notion to thwack you. What d' you mean by telling me my wife's gone? You're not sweet on her yourself, eh?"

Von Gerhard stifled an exclamation, and Orme turned quickly in his direction. "Who are you?" he asked. "Still another admirer? Jolly time you were having when I interrupted." He stared at Von Gerhard deliberately and coolly. A little frown of dislike came into his face. "You're a doctor, aren't you? I knew it. I can tell by the hands, and the eyes, and the skin, and the smell. Lived with 'em for ten years, damn them! Dawn, tell these fellows they're excused, will you? And by the way, you don't seem very happy to see me?"

I went up to him then, and laid my hand on his arm. "Peter, you don't understand. These two gentlemen have been all that is kind to me. I am happy to know that you are well again. Surely you do not expect me to be joyful at seeing you. All that pretense was left out of our lives long before your—illness. It hasn't been all roses for me since then, Peter. I've worked until I wanted to die with weariness. You know what this newspaper game is for a woman. It doesn't grow easier as she grows older and tireder."

"Oh, cut out the melodrama, Dawn," sneered Peter. "Have either of you fellows the makin's about you? Thanks. I'm famished for a smoke."

The worrying words of ten years ago rose automatically to my lips. "Aren't you smoking too much, Peter?" The tone was that of a harassed wife.

Peter stared. Then he laughed his short, mirthless little laugh. "By Jove! Dawn, I believe you're as much my wife now as you were ten years ago. I always said, you know, that you would have become a first-class nagger if you hadn't had such a keen sense of humor. That saved you." He turned his mocking eyes to Von Gerhard. "Doesn't it beat the devil, how these good women stick to a man, once they're married! There's a certain dog-like devotion about it that's touching."

There was a dreadful little silence. For the first time in my knowledge of him I saw a hot, painful red dyeing Blackie's sallow face. His eyes had a menace in their depths. Then, very quietly, Von Gerhard stepped forward and stopped directly before me.

"Dawn," he said, very softly and gently, "I retract my statement of an hour ago. If you will give me another chance to do as you asked me, I shall thank God for it all my life. There is no degradation in that. To live with this man—that is degradation. And I say you shall not suffer it."

I looked up into his face, and it had never seemed so dear to me. "The time for that is past," I said, my tone as calm and even as his own. "A man like you cannot burden himself with a derelict like me—mast gone, sails gone, water-logged, drifting. Five years from now you'll thank me for what I am saying now. My place is with this other wreck—tossed about by wind and weather until we both go down together." There came a sharp, insistent ring at the door-bell. No answering sound came from the regions above stairs. The ringing sounded again, louder than before.

"I'll be the Buttons," said Blackie, and disappeared into the hallway.

"Oh, yes, I've heard about you," came to our ears a moment later, in a high, clear voice—a dear, beloved voice that sent me flying to the door in an agony of hope.

"Norah!" I cried, "Norah! Norah! Norah!" And as her blessed arms closed about me the tears that had been denied me before came in a torrent of joy.

"There, there!" murmured she, patting my shoulder with those comforting mother-pats. "What's all this about? And why didn't somebody meet me? I telegraphed. You didn't get it? Well, I forgive you. Howdy-do, Peter? I suppose you are Peter. I hope you haven't been acting devilish again. That seems to be your specialty. Now don't smile that Mephistophelian smile at me. It doesn't frighten me. Von Gerhard, take him down to his hotel. I'm dying for my kimono and bed. And this child is trembling like a race-horse. Now run along, all of you. Things that look greenery-yallery at night always turn pink in the morning. Great Heavens! There's somebody calling down from the second-floor landing. It sounds like a landlady. Run, Dawn, and tell her your perfectly respectable sister has come. Peter! Von Gerhard! Mr. Blackie! Shoo!"

CHAPTER XIX

A TURN OF THE WHEEL

"You who were ever alert to befriend a man You who were ever the first to defend a man, You who had always the money to lend a man Down on his luck and hard up for a V, Sure you'll be playing a harp in beatitude (And a quare sight you will be in that attitude) Some day, where gratitude seems but a platitude, You'll find your latitude."

From my desk I could see Peter standing in the doorway of the news editor's room. I shut my eyes for a moment. Then I opened them again, quickly. No, it was not a dream. He was there, a slender, graceful, hateful figure, with the inevitable cigarette in his unsteady fingers—the expensive-looking, gold-tipped cigarette of the old days. Peter was Peter. Ten years had made little difference. There were queer little hollow places in his cheeks, and under the jaw-bone, and at the base of the head, and a flabby, parchment-like appearance about the skin. That was all that made him different from the Peter of the old days.

The thing had adjusted itself, as Norah had said it would. The situation that had filled me with loathing and terror the night of Peter's return had been transformed into quite a matter-of-fact and commonplace affair under Norah's deft management. And now I was back in harness again, and Peter was turning out brilliant political stuff at spasmodic intervals. He was not capable of any sustained effort. He never would be again; that was plain. He was growing restless and dissatisfied. He spoke of New York as though it were Valhalla. He said that he hadn't seen a pretty girl since he left Forty-second street. He laughed at Milwaukee's quaint German atmosphere. He sneered at our journalistic methods, and called the newspapers "country sheets," and was forever talking of the World, and the Herald, and the Sun, until the men at the Press Club fought shy of him. Norah had found quiet and comfortable quarters for Peter in a boarding-house near the lake, and just a square or two distant from my own boarding-house. He hated it cordially, as only the luxury-loving can hate a boarding-house, and threatened to leave daily.

"Let's go back to the big town, Dawn, old girl," he would say. "We're buried alive in this overgrown Dutch village. I came here in the first place on your account. Now it's up to you to get me out of it. Think of what New York means! Think of what I've been! And I can write as well as ever."

But I always shook my head. "We would not last a month in New York, Peter. New York has hurried on and left us behind. We're just two pieces of discard. We'll have to be content where we are."

"Content! In this silly hole! You must be mad!" Then, with one of his unaccountable changes of tone and topic, "Dawn, let me have some money. I'm strapped. If I had the time I'd get out some magazine stuff. Anything to get a little extra coin. Tell me, how does that little sport you call Blackie happen to have so much ready cash? I've never yet struck him for a loan that he hasn't obliged me. I think he's sweet on you, perhaps, and thinks he's doing you a sort of second-hand favor."

At times such as these all the old spirit that I had thought dead within me would rise up in revolt against this creature who was taking, from me my pride, my sense of honor, my friends. I never saw Von Gerhard now. Peter had refused outright to go to him for treatment, saying that he wasn't going to be poisoned by any cursed doctor, particularly not by one who had wanted to run away with his wife before his very eyes.

Sometimes I wondered how long this could go on. I thought of the old days with the Nirlangers; of Alma Pflugel's rose-encircled cottage; of Bennie; of the Knapfs; of the good-natured, uncouth aborigines, and their many kindnesses. I saw these dear people rarely now. Frau Nirlanger's resignation to her unhappiness only made me rebel more keenly against my own.

If only Peter could become well and strong again, I told myself, bitterly. If it were not for those blue shadows under his eyes, and the shrunken muscles, and the withered skin, I could leave him to live his life as he saw fit. But he was as dependent as a child, and as capricious. What was the end to be? I asked myself. Where was it all leading me?

And then, in a fearful and wonderful manner, my question was answered.

There came to my desk one day an envelope bearing the letter-head of the publishing house to which I had sent my story. I balanced it for a moment in my fingers, woman-fashion, wondering, hoping, surmising.

"Of course they can't want it," I told myself, in preparation for any disappointment that was in store for me. "They're sending it back. This is the letter that will tell me so."

And then I opened it. The words jumped out at me from the typewritten page. I crushed the paper in my hands, and rushed into Blackie's little office as I had been used to doing in the old days. He was at his desk, pipe in mouth. I shook his shoulder and flourished the letter wildly, and did a crazy little dance about his chair.

"They want it! They like it! Not only that, they want another, as soon as I can get it out. Think of it!"

Blackie removed his pipe from between his teeth and wiped his lips with the back of his hand. "I'm thinkin'," he said. "Anything t' oblige you. When you're through shovin' that paper into my face would you mind explainin' who wants what?"

"Oh, you're so stupid! So slow! Can't you see that I've written a real live book, and had it accepted, and that I am going to write another if I have to run away from a whole regiment of husbands to do it properly? Blackie, can't you see what it means!

Oh, Blackie, I know I'm maudlin in my joy, but forgive me. It's been so long since I've had the taste of it."

"Well, take a good chew while you got th'chance an' don't count too high on this first book business. I knew a guy who wrote a book once, an' he planned to take a trip to Europe on it, and build a house when he got home, and maybe a yacht or so, if he wasn't too rushed. Sa-a-ay, girl, w'en he got through gettin' those royalties for that book they'd dwindled down to fresh wall paper for the dinin'-room, and a new gas stove for his wife, an' not enough left over to take a trolley trip to Oshkosh on. Don't count too high."

"I'm not counting at all, Blackie, and you can't discourage me."

"Don't want to. But I'd hate to see you come down with a thud." Suddenly he sat up and a grin overspread his thin face. "Tell you what we'll do, girlie. We'll celebrate. Maybe it'll be the last time. Let's pretend this is six months ago, and everything's serene. You get your bonnet. I'll get the machine. It's too hot to work, anyway. We'll take a spin out to somewhere that's cool, and we'll order cold things to eat, and cold things to drink, and you can talk about yourself till you're tired. You'll have to take it out on somebody, an' it might as well be me."

Five minutes later, with my hat in my hand, I turned to find Peter at my elbow.

"Want to talk to you," he said, frowning.

"Sorry, Peter, but I can't stop. Won't it do later?"

"No. Got an assignment? I'll go with you."

"N-not exactly, Peter. The truth is, Blackie has taken pity on me and has promised to take me out for a spin, just to cool off. It has been so insufferably hot."

Peter turned away. "Count me in on that," he said, over his shoulder.

"But I can't, Peter," I cried. "It isn't my party. And anyway—"

Peter turned around, and there was an ugly glow in his eyes and an ugly look on his face, and a little red ridge that I had not noticed before seemed to burn itself across his forehead. "And anyway, you don't want me, eh? Well, I'm going. I'm not going to have my wife chasing all over the country with strange men. Remember, you're not the giddy grass widdy you used to be. You can take me, or stay at home, understand?"

His voice was high-pitched and quavering. Something in his manner struck a vague terror to my heart. "Why, Peter, if you care that much I shall be glad to have you go. So will Blackie, I am sure. Come, we'll go down now. He'll be waiting for us."

Blackie's keen, clever mind grasped the situation as soon as he saw us together. His dark face was illumined by one of his rare smiles. "Coming with us, Orme? Do you good. Pile into the tonneau, you two, and hang on to your hair. I'm going to smash the law."

Peter sauntered up to the steering-wheel. "Let me drive," he said. "I'm not bad at it."

"Nix with the artless amateur," returned Blackie. "This ain't no demonstration car. I drive my own little wagon when I go riding, and I intend to until I take my last ride, feet first."

Peter muttered something surly and climbed into the front seat next to Blackie, leaving me to occupy the tonneau in solitary state.

Peter began to ask questions—dozens of them, which Blackie answered, patiently and fully. I could not hear all that they said, but I saw that Peter was urging Blackie to greater speed, and that Blackie was explaining that he must first leave the crowded streets behind. Suddenly Peter made a gesture in the direction of the wheel, and said something in a high, sharp voice. Blackie's answer was quick and decidedly in the negative. The next instant Peter Orme rose in his place and leaning forward and upward, grasped the wheel that was in Blackie's hands. The car swerved sickeningly. I noticed, dully, that Blackie did not go white as novelists say men do in moments of horror. A dull red flush crept to the very base of his neck. With a twist of his frail body he tried to throw off Peter's hands. I remember leaning over the back of the seat and trying to pull Peter back as I realized that it was a madman with whom we were dealing. Nothing seemed real. It was ridiculously like the things one sees in the moving picture theaters. I felt no fear.

"Sit down, Orme!" Blackie yelled. "You'll ditch us! Dawn! God!—"

We shot down a little hill. Two wheels were lifted from the ground. The machine was poised in the air for a second before it crashed into the ditch and turned over completely, throwing me clear, but burying Blackie and Peter under its weight of steel and wood and whirring wheels.

I remember rising from the ground, and sinking back again and rising once more to run forward to where the car lay in the ditch, and tugging at that great frame of steel with crazy, futile fingers. Then I ran screaming down the road toward a man who was tranquilly working in a field nearby.

CHAPTER XX

BLACKIE'S VACATION COMES

The shabby blue office coat hangs on the hook in the little sporting room where Blackie placed it. No one dreams of moving it. There it dangles, out at elbows, disreputable, its pockets burned from many a hot pipe thrust carelessly into them, its cuffs frayed, its lapels bearing the marks of cigarette, paste-pot and pen.

It is that faded old garment, more than anything else, which makes us fail to realize that its owner will never again slip into its comfortable folds. We cannot believe that a lifeless rag like that can triumph over the man of flesh and blood and nerves and sympathies. With what contempt do we look upon those garments during our lifetime! And how they live on, defying time, long, long after we have been gathered to our last rest.

In some miraculous manner Blackie had lived on for two days after that ghastly ride. Peter had been killed instantly, the doctors said. They gave no hope for Blackie. My escape with but a few ridiculous bruises and scratches was due, they said, to the fact that I had sat in the tonneau. I heard them all, in a stupor of horror and grief, and wondered what plan Fate had in store for me, that I alone should have been spared. Norah and Max came, and took things in charge, and I saw Von Gerhard, but all three appeared dim and shadowy, like figures in a mist. When I closed my eyes I could see Peter's tense figure bending over Blackie at the wheel, and heard his labored breathing as he struggled in his mad fury, and felt again the helpless horror that had come to me as we swerved off the road and into the ditch below, with

Blackie, rigid and desperate, still clinging to the wheel. I lived it all over and over in my mind. In the midst of the blackness I heard a sentence that cleared the fog from my mind, and caused me to raise myself from my pillows.

Some one—Norah, I think—had said that Blackie was conscious, and that he was asking for some of the men at the office, and for me. For me! I rose and dressed, in spite of Norah's protests. I was quite well, I told them. I must see him. I shook them off with trembling fingers and when they saw that I was quite determined they gave in, and Von Gerhard telephoned to the hospital to learn the hour at which I might meet the others who were to see Blackie for a brief moment.

I met them in the stiff little waiting room of he hospital—Norberg, Deming, Schmidt, Holt—men who had known him from the time when they had yelled, "Heh, boy!" at him when they wanted their pencils sharpened. Awkwardly we followed the fleet-footed nurse who glided ahead of us down the wide hospital corridors, past doorways through which we caught glimpses of white beds that were no whiter than the faces that lay on the pillows. We came at last into a very still and bright little room where Blackie lay.

Had years passed over his head since I saw him last? The face that tried to smile at us from the pillow was strangely wizened and old. It was as though a withering blight had touched it. Only the eyes were the same. They glowed in the sunken face, beneath the shock of black hair, with a startling luster and brilliancy.

I do not know what pain he suffered. I do not know what magic medicine gave him the strength to smile at us, dying as he was even then.

"Well, what do you know about little Paul Dombey?" he piped in a high, thin voice. The shock of relief was too much. We giggled hysterically, then stopped short and looked at each other, like scared and naughty children.

"Sa-a-ay, boys and girls, cut out the heavy thinking parts. Don't make me do all the social stunts. What's the news? What kind of a rotten cotton sportin' sheet is that dub Callahan gettin' out? Who won to-day—Cubs or Pirates? Norberg, you goat, who pinned that purple tie on you?"

He was so like the Blackie we had always known that we were at our ease immediately. The sun shone in at the window, and some one laughed a little laugh somewhere down the corridor, and Deming, who is Irish, plunged into a droll description of a brand-new office boy who had arrived that day.

"S'elp me, Black, the kid wears spectacles and a Norfolk suit, and low-cut shoes with bows on 'em. On the square he does. Looks like one of those Boston infants you see in the comic papers. I don't believe he's real. We're saving him until you get back, if the kids in the alley don't chew him up before that time."

An almost imperceptible shade passed over Blackie's face. He closed his eyes for a moment. Without their light his countenance was ashen, and awful.

A nurse in stripes and cap appeared in the doorway. She looked keenly at the little figure in the bed. Then she turned to us.

"You must go now," she said. "You were just to see him for a minute or two, you know."

Blackie summoned the wan ghost of a smile to his lips. "Guess you guys ain't got th' stimulatin' effect that a bunch of live wires ought to have. Say, Norberg, tell that fathead, Callahan, if he don't keep the third drawer t' the right in my desk locked, th' office kids'll swipe all the roller rink passes surest thing you know."

"I'll—tell him, Black," stammered Norberg, and turned away.

They said good-by, awkwardly enough. Not one of them that did not owe him an unpayable debt of gratitude. Not one that had not the memory of some secret kindness stored away in his heart. It was Blackie who had furnished the money that had sent Deming's sick wife west. It had been Blackie who had rescued Schmidt time and again when drink got a stranglehold. Blackie had always said: "Fire Schmidt! Not much! Why, Schmidt writes better stuff drunk than all the rest of the bunch sober." And Schmidt would be granted another reprieve by the Powers that Were.

Suddenly Blackie beckoned the nurse in the doorway. She came swiftly and bent over him.

"Gimme two minutes more, that's a good nursie. There's something I want to say t' this dame. It's de rigger t' hand out last messages, ain't it?"

The nurse looked at me, doubtfully. "But you're not to excite yourself."

"Sa-a-ay, girl, this ain't goin' t' be no scene from East Lynne. Be a good kid. The rest of the bunch can go."

And so, when the others had gone, I found myself seated at the side of his bed, trying to smile down at him. I knew that there must be nothing to excite him. But the words on my lips would come.

"Blackie," I said, and I struggled to keep my voice calm and emotionless, "Blackie, forgive me. It is all my fault—my wretched fault."

"Now, cut that," interrupted Blackie. "I thought that was your game. That's why I said I wanted t' talk t' you. Now, listen. Remember my tellin' you, a few weeks ago, 'bout that vacation I was plannin'? This is it, only it's come sooner than I expected, that's all. I seen two three doctor guys about it. Your friend Von Gerhard was one of 'em. They didn't tell me t' take no ocean trip this time. Between 'em, they decided my vacation would come along about November, maybe. Well, I beat 'em to it, that's all. Sa-a-ay, girl, I ain't kickin'. You can't live on your nerves and expect t' keep goin'. Sooner or later you'll be suein' those same nerves for non-support. But, kid, ain't it a shame that I got to go out in a auto smashup, in these days when even a airship exit don't make a splash on the front page!"

The nervous brown hand was moving restlessly over the covers. Finally it met my hand, and held it in a tense little grip.

"We've been good pals, you and me, ain't we, kid?"

"Yes, Blackie."

"Ain't regretted it none?"

"Regretted it! I am a finer, truer, better woman for having known you, Blackie."

He gave a little contented sigh at that, and his eyes closed. When he opened them the old, whimsical smile wrinkled his face.

"This is where I get off at. It ain't been no long trip, but sa-a-ay, girl, I've enjoyed every mile of the road. All kinds of scenery—all kinds of lan'scape—plain—fancy—uphill—downhill—"

I leaned forward, fearfully.

"Not—yet," whispered Blackie. "Say Dawn—in the story books—they—always—are strong on the—good-by kiss, what?"

And as the nurse appeared in the doorway again, disapproval on her face, I stooped and gently pressed my lips to the pain-lined cheek.

CHAPTER XXI

HAPPINESS

We laid Peter to rest in that noisy, careless, busy city that he had loved so well, and I think his cynical lips would have curled in a bitterly amused smile, and his somber eyes would have flamed into sudden wrath if he could have seen how utterly and completely New York had forgotten Peter Orme. He had been buried alive ten years before—and Newspaper Row has no faith in resurrections. Peter Orme was not even a memory. Ten years is an age in a city where epochs are counted by hours.

Now, after two weeks of Norah's loving care, I was back in the pretty little city by the lake. I had come to say farewell to all those who had filled my life so completely in that year. My days of newspaper work were over. The autumn and winter would be spent at Norah's, occupied with hours of delightful, congenial work, for the second book was to be written in the quiet peace of my own little Michigan town. Von Gerhard was to take his deferred trip to Vienna in the spring, and I knew that I was to go with him. The thought filled my heart with a great flood of happiness.

Together Von Gerhard and I had visited Alma Pflugel's cottage, and the garden was blooming in all its wonder of color and scent as we opened the little gate and walked up the worn path. We found them in the cool shade of the arbor, the two women sewing, Bennie playing with the last wonderful toy that Blackie had given him. They made a serene and beautiful picture there against the green canopy of the leaves. We spoke of Frau Nirlanger, and of Blackie, and of the strange snarl of events which had at last been unwound to knit a close friendship between us. And when I had kissed them and walked for the last time in many months up the flower-bordered path, the scarlet and pink, and green and gold of that wonderful garden swam in a mist before my eyes.

Frau Nirlanger was next. When we spoke of Vienna she caught her breath sharply.

"Vienna!" she repeated, and the longing in her voice was an actual pain. "Vienna! Gott! Shall I ever see it again? Vienna! My boy is there. Perhaps—"

"Perhaps," I said, gently. "Stranger things have happened. Perhaps if I could see them, and talk to them—if I could tell them—they might be made to understand. I haven't been a newspaper reporter all these years without acquiring a golden gift of persuasiveness. Perhaps—who knows?—we may meet again in Vienna. Stranger things have happened."

Frau Nirlanger shook her head with a little hopeless sigh. "You do not know Vienna; you do not know the iron strength of caste, and custom and stiff-necked pride. I am dead in Vienna. And the dead should rest in peace."

It was late in the afternoon when Von Gerhard and I turned the corner which led to the building that held the Post. I had saved that for the last.

"I hope that heaven is not a place of golden streets, and twanging harps and angel choruses," I said, softly. "Little, nervous, slangy, restless Blackie, how bored and ill at ease he would be in such a heaven! How lonely, without his old black pipe, and his checked waistcoats, and his diamonds, and his sporting extra. Oh, I hope they have all those comforting, everyday things up there, for Blackie's sake."

"How you grew to understand him in that short year," mused Von Gerhard. "I sometimes used to resent the bond between you and this little Blackie whose name was always on your tongue."

"Ah, that was because you did not comprehend. It is given to very few women to know the beauty of a man's real friendship.

That was the bond between Blackie and me. To me he was a comrade, and to him I was a good-fellow girl—one to whom he could talk without excusing his pipe or cigarette. Love and love-making were things to bring a kindly, amused chuckle from Blackie."

Von Gerhard was silent. Something in his silence held a vague irritation for me. I extracted a penny from my purse, and placed it in his hand.

"I was thinking," he said, "that none are so blind as those who will not see."

"I don't understand," I said, puzzled.

"That is well," answered Von Gerhard, as we entered the building. "That is as it should be." And he would say nothing more.

The last edition of the paper had been run off for the day. I had purposely waited until the footfalls of the last departing reporter should have ceased to echo down the long corridor. The city room was deserted except for one figure bent over a pile of papers and proofs. Norberg, the city editor, was the last to leave, as always. His desk light glowed in the darkness of the big room, and his typewriter alone awoke the echoes.

As I stood in the doorway he peered up from beneath his green eye-shade, and waved a cloud of smoke away with the palm of his hand.

"That you, Mrs. Orme?" he called out. "Lord, we've missed you! That new woman can't write an obituary, and her teary tales sound like they were carved with a cold chisel. When are you coming back?"

"I'm not coming back," I replied. "I've come to say good-by to you and—Blackie."

Norberg looked up quickly. "You feel that way, too? Funny. So do the rest of us. Sometimes I think we are all half sure that it is only another of his impish tricks, and that some morning he will pop open the door of the city room here and call out, 'Hello, slaves! Been keepin' m' memory green?'"

I held out my hand to him, gratefully. He took it in his great palm, and a smile dimpled his plump cheeks. "Going to blossom into a regular little writer, h'm? Well, they say it's a paying game when you get the hang of it. And I guess you've got it. But if ever you feel that you want a real thrill—a touch of the old satisfying newspaper feeling—a sniff of wet ink—the music of some editorial cussing—why come up here and I'll give you the hottest assignment on my list, if I have to take it away from Deming's very notebook."

When I had thanked him I crossed the hall and tried the door of the sporting editor's room. Von Gerhard was waiting for me far down at the other end of the corridor. The door opened and I softly entered and shut it again. The little room was dim, but in the half-light I could see that Callahan had changed something—had shoved a desk nearer the window, or swung the typewriter over to the other side. I resented it. I glanced up at the corner where the shabby old office coat had been wont to hang. There it dangled, untouched, just as he had left it. Callahan had not dared to change that. I tip-toed over to the corner and touched it gently with my fingers. A light pall of dust had settled over the worn little garment, but I knew each worn place, each ink-spot, each scorch or burn from pipe or cigarette. I passed my hands over it reverently and gently, and then, in the dimness of that quiet little room I laid my cheek against the rough cloth, so that the scent of the old black pipe came back to me once more, and a new spot appeared on the coat sleeve—a damp, salt spot. Blackie would have hated my doing that. But he was not there to see, and one spot more or less did not matter; it was such a grimy, disreputable old coat.

"Dawn!" called Von Gerhard softly, outside the door. "Dawn! Coming, Kindchen?"

I gave the little coat a parting pat. "Goodby," I whispered, under my breath, and turned toward the door.

"Coming!" I called, aloud.

CPSIA information can be obtained
at www.ICGtesting.com
Printed in the USA
LVHW041241270123
737933LV00003B/762